Mariah was the last woman he should be interested in.

A reporter who had the power to destroy his peaceful life.

But Jackson had to admit he enjoyed the feel of her arms locked around his waist as they rode out to the fence line. He stared at the damage. The fence had obviously been cut. By whom? He didn't have any enemies. But for several weeks there had been incidents that made him uneasy.

"This repair might take a while," he told her. "Why don't you go down to the creek?"

He watched her walk away, but he put the brakes on his thoughts. *Don't think about the greenhorn reporter. She'll be leaving in a few days anyway.* Jackson shook his head. That's why he didn't want women on the ranch. They were a distraction. Nothing but trouble.

He worked on the repair till a loud crack echoed over the hills. Jackson jumped, nicking his finger on a barb. Gunfire?

Another blast ripped the quiet, followed by a scream.

Mariah!

VICKIE McDONOUGH

is an award-winning and bestselling author of over thirty published books and novellas. She grew up wanting to marry a rancher, but instead, she married a computer geek who is scared of horses. She now lives out her dreams in her fictional stories about ranchers, cowboys, lawmen and others living in the West. She's a wife of almost forty years, mother of four grown sons and one daughter-in-law, and is grandma to a feisty eight-year-old girl. When she's not writing, Vickie enjoys reading, buying cool things for her booth in an antique mall, watching movies and traveling. To learn more about Vickie's books or to sign up for her newsletter, visit her website: www.vickiemcdonough.com. You can also find Vickie on Facebook and Twitter.

RANCHER UNDER FIRE

VICKIE McDONOUGH

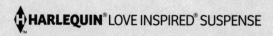

HARLEQUIN® LOVE INSPIRED® SUSPENSE

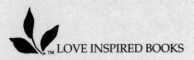

LOVE INSPIRED BOOKS

Recycling programs
for this product may
not exist in your area.

ISBN-13: 978-0-373-44623-0

RANCHER UNDER FIRE

Copyright © 2014 by Vickie McDonough

www.Harlequin.com

Printed in U.S.A.

But those who hope in the Lord
will renew their strength.
They will soar on wings like eagles;
they will run and not grow weary,
they will walk and not be faint.
—*Isaiah* 40:31

To my agent, Chip MacGregor.
If not for Chip, this book would never have
happened. Thanks for pushing me and
opening doors that give life to *Rancher Under Fire*.

ONE

Mariah Reyes had to face the facts—she was lost. Hours of wandering on the desolate country roads of Northeastern Oklahoma had left her more confused than a chameleon in a bowl of Skittles.

She checked for oncoming cars—not that she'd seen more than one in the past half hour—then reached for the map on the passenger's seat. She peeked down at the line she'd drawn before leaving home that showed the way to Angelfire Ranch, but it didn't help. Glancing up, she jerked the steering wheel to the right to get her car back in her lane and willed her pulse to return to normal.

"This is crazy." She slowed the car, pulled onto the gravel shoulder and searched her purse for her phone. Maybe she could find her way using the built-in GPS and maps. She turned it on and opened the map app. She'd already plugged in the address to Jackson Durant's ranch, but she hadn't wanted to risk driving while trying to follow the tiny GPS dot on her phone.

She studied the barren winter wilderness while she waited for the map to load. Tall, yellow grass fluttered in the wind, and the few leaves still clinging to the almost-bald trees waved at her. The land here wasn't as flat as the Dallas area, and there were more trees, but the emptiness of the countryside after the busyness of the big city left her feeling isolated.

She checked her phone. With only one bar on her cell, the map wouldn't load. "That's great." Mariah tossed the phone onto the passenger's seat and blew out a sigh. So much for modern technology.

Now what?

She'd passed a farm several miles back, but she hated asking for help. She shifted the car in gear and drove forward. Just a few more miles, and if she didn't find Angelfire Ranch, she'd turn around or ask someone for directions.

Fifteen minutes later, she pulled into a parking lot containing half a dozen trucks and a single gray sedan. She looped her arm through her purse straps and read the name of the establishment made from cement blocks painted an icky avocado-green: Tank Up—Gas and Bar. She shook her head. "Only in Oklahoma."

A Coke and some chocolate would do a lot to improve her mood. She grabbed her map, pressed the remote to lock the car and headed into the store. Loud music, smoke and the odor of burned pizza greeted her.

A slim clerk dressed in denim, boots and a cowboy hat nodded. "Howdy, ma'am." His gaze dropped to the map in her hand. "Can I he'p you find somethin'?"

She smiled. "Just let me grab a Coke first."

Mariah surveyed her surroundings—something she did as a habit. Probably the reporter in her wanting to know everything that was happening. The right side of the building housed a small convenience store while the left opened up to tables, chairs and a bar on the far wall. Neon signs shone through the cloud of smoke that hovered above a table where four men played cards and drank beer. The country music blaring from an old jukebox in the far corner whined a song she didn't recognize. The buzz of conversation stopped, and the men at the table, along with another guy talking to the bartender, turned to gawk at her.

Mariah spun around, snatched a candy bar off the rack and made a beeline for the soda fountain. Thanks to her father, men made her nervous, especially ones who were indulging in liquor. She never knew what to expect from them. Three years as an investigative reporter had boosted her courage and made her much more outgoing, but being the only woman with seven men—some of whom were drinking—increased her anxiety.

She filled a disposable cup then hurried to the counter and paid for her items. She eyed a slice of cheese pizza in a warmer behind the clerk but decided she didn't need the carbs. Glancing back at the clerk, she fished her wallet from her purse. "Could you please tell me how to find Angelfire Ranch?"

The young cowboy smiled. "Sure thang, ma'am. Just head north four miles or so until you see a broken-down hay baler in a field then turn right. You'll see the big Angelfire sign after a few minutes. Cain't miss it."

She wanted to ask what a hay baler looked like, but several of the men from the table had risen and were ambling her way. Mariah gathered her things and rushed out the door. She didn't breathe a sigh of relief until she turned her Mustang onto the road again.

She made note of the mileage so she could tell when she'd traveled four miles. At least she was closer to Angelfire Ranch than she'd thought.

A motion in the rearview mirror snagged Mariah's attention. A black truck—no two—spun out of the store's parking lot and were approaching fast.

Mariah pressed down the gas pedal, keeping watch on the odometer, the road and the trucks. Did they just happen to leave at the same time? Or were they following her?

She glanced at the speedometer—seven miles per hour

over the speed limit—and the nearest truck was still closing the space between them. Mariah grasped the wheel
harder, and her pulse jumped into overdrive. Just when
she thought the first truck would ram her, it whizzed into
the other lane and passed her. She glanced in the passenger window of the second truck as it also zoomed by, but
the tinting was too dark for her to see through.

She relaxed her grip on the wheel and blew out an irritated breath. "Show-offs!"

As the second black truck passed her, she looked for the
tag number, but the lower half of the vehicle was covered in
mud. Suddenly, the truck swerved back into her lane, and
the taillights lit up. The gap between her car and the pickup
narrowed. Mariah slammed on her brakes and swerved into
the other lane, tires squealing. A quick glance revealed no
oncoming traffic. Her left rear tire dropped off the tarred
edge, and she struggled to get it back on the road. Gravel
chunked against the underbelly of her car. She jerked the
wheel to the right, bumped up onto the asphalt and slowed
to a stop on the center line. The truck sped down the road
and disappeared around the corner.

Mariah's heart pounded.

What just happened?

Had that driver deliberately tried to run her off the road?

Blowing out a breath, Mariah checked for traffic then
pulled onto the right side of the road again. She wasn't eas-
ily scared, but the randomness of the attack left her trembling. Maybe the driver had drunk too much liquor—or
maybe mistaken her for someone else. Or maybe he was
hotdogging. That was the only thing that made sense.

She glanced at the odometer, glad to see she had only
another mile until the turnoff to Jackson Durant's ranch.
She hoped he was ready for her, because she aimed to get
the real story about why he quit football in the midst of an

undefeated season, not the fluff Where Are They Now? piece her editor wanted.

In the field to her right, she spied a rusty heap of equipment, which must be the hay baler since it was the only farm apparatus around. The road to Angelfire stretched out past the end of the fence line. "Finally!"

A movement straight ahead caught her eye. A black truck crept over the next hill, which was several hundred yards past the turnoff. Mariah's heart jolted. Was it the same truck that had nearly caused her to crash?

She wasn't waiting around to find out. She pressed on the gas, but as the Mustang charged forward like a thoroughbred from a starting gate, so did the truck. Mariah eyed the distance to the turnoff, keeping a death grip on the steering wheel. Just a few more yards.

The truck veered into her lane, barreling toward her.

Mariah swung the wheel a bit early, hoping she didn't land in the ditch. She had to make this turn. Her tires squealed as the rear end of her car swept around the corner then fishtailed. She righted it just as the truck reached the turn. Mariah stomped the gas pedal to the floor. The store clerk had said she'd see the sign to Angelfire Ranch in a few minutes, but she reached it in one. She slowed down to make the turn onto the ranch's gravel road.

Would the truck follow her onto private property?

If it did, she'd be ready. This was one driver she'd take delight in using her Taser on.

Jackson Durant hugged his daughter, enjoying her laughter.

Hailey released her hold on his neck and pushed back to look him in the face. "Toss me up again, Daddy."

"One more time. Then we need to get back to work." He lowered her to the ground, and Hailey squatted down then jumped. Jackson lifted her and pitched her up a couple of feet into the air over his head. He wouldn't be able to toss his six-year-old like this much longer. He lowered her back down, amid girlish giggles, and squeezed her shoulder. "Time to get busy."

He retrieved the yearling he'd tied to the paddock fence and led her out into the yard. The black filly would make a good saddle horse one day, but she still needed some work.

"Can I lead her?"

Jackson peered down at his daughter's pixie face, remembering again how close he had come to losing her the day she was born. A deep ache gutted his insides even worse than the pain he'd felt when he walked away from quarterbacking an undefeated team on its way to the Super Bowl. He couldn't imagine—didn't want to imagine—what his life would be like without his daughter.

Every day her brown eyes and sweet smile looked more and more like her mother's. Would he be reminded of his wife's betrayal for the rest of his life, just by looking into his daughter's face?

As if sensing his troubled thoughts, Baron licked Jackson's hand. He reached down and patted the border collie's black-and-white head. No, Hailey might look like Misty, but his daughter didn't have her mother's shallow character. Once again he slammed the lid on the anger bubbling up at the thought of Misty's disloyalty. Though the familiar pain had numbed a bit over the years, whenever he thought of his deceased wife, it threatened to rise to the surface again, disturbing his peace with God.

"Hello…Da-addy?" Stretching onto the tiptoes of her tan cowboy boots, Hailey waved her hand back and forth in front of his face.

The black filly on the other end of the lead rope in Jackson's hand shook her head and snorted, wary of his daughter's flapping arm. "Hey, settle down," he said to both females. Grasping the horse's halter, he stared at his daughter. "Hailey, you know better than to make any sudden movements around these green broke horses."

Nostrils flaring and the whites of her eyes showing, the filly attempted to jerk her head free of his hold.

Jackson held the small horse secure, rubbing her neck. "Shh. You're okay."

"Daddy?" Hailey patted Jackson's stomach. "So…can I lead her around?"

"Just a minute." Jackson observed the black filly for a few moments. When she quieted, he released her halter but hung on to the coiled lead rope. The horse ducked her head, nibbling the ankle-high winter grass at his feet.

He patted the filly's shoulder. Had she calmed enough for Hailey to handle her? He breathed a deep sigh. Did every father wrestle with the issues he did, or was his daily struggle to find a balance with Hailey and duties at the ranch related to his being an overprotective single dad? He wanted to keep his daughter safe but not smother her. His gaze lifted across the ranch yard to the horses grazing peacefully in the pasture. His daughter loved horses as much as he, and she had never been afraid of them, not even as a toddler. Though he wanted to hold her back until she was older— and bigger—Hailey knew how to handle horses, even if her childishness sometimes overpowered her sensibilities. He patted his daughter's back. "I guess you can lead the filly for a while, but don't make any sudden movements, and don't go too far in case you need me."

"Yip—" Hailey slapped her palm to her mouth, halting her high-pitched cheer. Her gaze darted to the filly and back to him as she lowered her hand. "Sorry. I'll be quieter."

Chuckling, he handed the lead rope to his daughter. What was the point in trying to keep her away from the horses? She loved them and was a natural. Pride swelled in his chest as he watched Hailey curl up the nylon rope with the skill of one raised her whole life on a ranch. Holding the coil in one hand, she clutched the lead just below the snap and walked the yearling down the gravel drive.

"C'mon, girl. You and me's gonna be buddies." Baron trotted along behind them for a few feet, but then he turned and moseyed back to Jackson's side.

Shoving his hands in his pockets, Jackson scanned the well-kept ranch. The gray single-story house provided a cozy escape from the hot Oklahoma summers and chilly winters. His new red barn, complete with modern amenities like a sprinkler system and a bathroom with a shower, had stalls for twelve horses and was the envy of his neighbors. Across the rolling hills, quarter horses grazed lazily in the unusually warm December weather. His chest swelled as gratitude filled his heart—but then he remembered the dark shadows of recent days, and his gaze lifted. *Thank You, Lord, for allowing me to realize my dream of owning this ranch. Please help me figure out the root of the problems plaguing me lately. They can't be coincidences.*

Pursing his lips, he watched Hailey turn the filly and head toward him. So far his problems hadn't caused her any harm, except for upsetting her. He considered all the things that had happened in the past few weeks—broken fences, missing equipment, sick horses. Was he simply having a run of bad luck?

"Don't ya think she'll make a good barrel racer? I'm gonna name her Sabrina."

"That's a fine name." He smiled. Hailey had to name every horse that passed through their ranch, whether it stayed for a week or forever. While at Angelfire Ranch, the animals were treated like family. Sometimes the rodeo owners and other people he sold the horses to kept the names his daughter had given them and sometimes they changed them, but Hailey didn't care as long as she gave them their first one.

The familiar ta-dump, ta-dump of tires crossing the cattle

guard pulled his gaze down the long gravel drive. Though people frequented the ranch often, he wasn't expecting anyone today. He studied the approaching vehicle—a sports car that was going far too fast.

He started toward his daughter. "Hailey, bring the filly back. Right now."

Hailey stopped in the middle of the road and stared at the car, barreling toward her. Jackson increased his pace. His daughter tugged the prancing horse off the road and onto the dried winter grass. The filly pawed the ground. The closer the sports car came, the more agitated she grew.

Baron barked. Jackson broke into a run. A shrill whinny rent the air as the black filly reared, her front hooves pawing the air just inches above Hailey's head. Jackson's heart took a dive. He raced toward her, but his legs felt as if they were encased in cement.

"Let go! Hailey! Let go of the rope." His words sounded hollow, as if shouted down a long, narrow tunnel.

Sabrina bolted, yanking his daughter to the ground and dragging her back toward the road as the car maneuvered a bend and headed straight for them. Baron raced for the front of the horse, as if to cut her off and turn her back. The driver blasted the horn. The car skidded and swerved, sending a dusty cloud of gravel and dirt over filly and dog. Tires spun, chunking pebbles against the car's underbelly, and the Mustang veered to the right as the driver spun around trying to miss a large maple tree. Metal and fiberglass crunched against wood as the car lost the fight.

Heart pounding, Jackson slowed as he reached Hailey and lifted her to her feet, pressing her against him. That car had come so close to hitting her. "You okay, sweetie? Are you hurt?"

Hailey's mumbled response warmed his blue denim shirt, but he couldn't make out the words. His daughter pushed against his belly, and he reluctantly released her.

"I couldn't breathe, Daddy." She gulped in several gasps of air, then glanced at the rope burns on her palms. "I tried to hold on so Sabrina wouldn't get away. I wasn't scared, but I couldn't hang on."

He scanned his daughter's face and body to make sure she wasn't injured then released the breath he'd been holding. Her denim jacket was dust-covered but had probably saved her from scraping or bruising her arms. With his sleeve, he wiped dirt off her chin, relieved that she hadn't cut it. A few minor rope burns reddened her palms, but otherwise she looked fine.

With his hands shaking and heart ricocheting around his chest like a racquetball on a court, he was in worse shape than his daughter. Not quite believing she was unharmed, he asked again, "You're really not hurt anywhere besides your hands?"

"I'm fine, but that car's not. And Sabrina's gettin' away."

He glanced in the direction Hailey pointed. Still galloping and flipping chunks of dirt behind her, Sabrina had almost reached the ranch's entrance. The blue lead rope flapped in the air like a pennant. Baron had given up the chase and trotted toward them, tongue hanging out.

With the danger past, Jackson looked skyward. *Thank You, Lord, for protecting my little girl.*

Ruffling his daughter's hair, he said, "Don't worry about Sabrina, pun'kin. We'll catch her or one of our neighbors will."

Draping his arm around Hailey's shoulders, he turned toward the wrecked vehicle. Hissing steam seeped from the metallic blue Mustang now hugging his silver-maple tree.

He clenched his jaw, fighting his anger. Even his years of professional football training hadn't prepared him for the rage coursing through him at the person who'd put his daughter's life in danger with such reckless driving. If not for his Christian faith, he'd march forward and punch the driver's nose. What kind of idiot raced up the drive of a horse ranch?

Jackson took a deep breath and unclenched his fist. He ought to be concerned about the driver, but at the moment, thoughts of his daughter's near miss overpowered any compassion he might have.

"Cool car," Hailey said. "Well, it *was* cool."

With an eerie groan, the door creaked opened. Two small feet clad in navy pumps appeared below the door. A feminine, well-manicured hand grasped the top of the window frame, and a woman's brunette head popped up above the dark tinted glass of the driver's window. Wariness churned deep in Jackson's belly. What was a woman doing here?

After a moment she stepped out from behind the car door and glared down the road. "That horse ran right in front of me. Look what it did to my car."

"If you hadn't been driving so fast, you wouldn't have spooked her and caused her to bolt." Jackson yanked his black Stetson off and smacked it against his leg, wishing he could follow Sabrina and be rid of this unwanted visitor.

"Uh-oh, there goes another hat," Hailey mumbled. "That lady's in trouble now."

He cringed at her comment. He'd lost count of the number of Western hats he'd gone through as a result of trying to control his temper. He liked this particular one and aimed to keep it awhile. Slapping it back on his head, he marched forward.

"Listen, lady, your driving nearly got my daughter killed." Hands clamped to his waist, he glared down into the woman's startled black eyes.

She took only a second to recover from her surprised reaction. "Me? What are you talking about?" She swiped her hand toward the crumpled hood. "Look at my car!" Sobering suddenly, she turned toward the road again. "Did you see that truck?"

Jackson glanced down the road, wondering about her random change of topics. "What truck?"

The moment of vulnerability disappeared as the woman tossed her dark mane over her shoulders, then tilted up her face and glared back at him, ebony eyes flashing. "I never even saw your daughter, and that horse did run right at me." She reached one hand to the car door and white-knuckled the window frame. Her expression softened. "Is your daughter okay?"

Jackson nodded, his heart still beating faster than normal at the close call.

Hailey skidded to a stop beside him. "Daddy, did the lady get hurt?"

He smiled at his daughter and brushed his hand across her head, and then Jackson studied the woman for a moment. At six foot two, he normally towered over most females, but this one appeared to be less than a half foot shorter than him. Her olive complexion and black eyes verified her Hispanic heritage. Wisps of dark brown hair curled around her oval face, giving her a softer appearance than Jackson expected from such a fireball.

"Look. I'm sorry. I really didn't see your daughter—or the horse—until it ran in front of me. It's just that…" She glanced toward the ranch's entrance again then pursed her lips. "Never mind."

The woman lifted a finger to her nose and a tiny sneeze squeaked past her pink lips.

Jackson blinked. He'd never heard such a feminine sound before.

"My, there's a lot of dust out here." She waved her hand in front of her face.

"Yeah." Jackson straightened. "Especially when someone drives too fast and fishtails on the gravel." Or when it didn't rain for weeks, but he let that thought slide.

The woman hiked her chin; the fire in her eyes brightened. "Sorry if I was going too fast. You don't exactly have a speed-limit sign posted. I've been driving up and down these country roads for hours, trying to find this place. Not to mention—" She jerked a tissue out of the pocket of her navy business suit and stuffed it under her pert nose just as another sneeze squeaked out.

"Why didn't you stop and ask somebody? Everyone around these parts knows where Angelfire Ranch is." Why did men always get blamed for not asking directions when women were just as bad?

Her chin lifted again. "I had a map. But obviously whoever faxed it to me didn't know how to draw intelligent directions." She ducked into her car, grabbed a piece of paper, then waved it in his face. "See?"

Jackson instantly recognized the map to his ranch printed on Angelfire letterhead. An ominous feeling, like overthrowing the final pass that would have won his team the play-off game, settled in his gut.

"Why don't y'all quit fussin'?" Hailey held out her hand to the woman and smiled. "I'm Hailey Durant. This is my daddy. Did you know he was a famous football player?"

The woman blinked at him, and then the color left her cheeks, leaving it to resemble the milky coffee Hailey occasionally drank. "You're J. D. Durant—ex–Texas Tornados quarterback?"

"Folks around here call me Jackson." He gave Hailey a stern look. He should have scolded his daughter for her outspokenness, but his mind was too busy racing, trying to figure out what business this citified woman had with him. Today was Thursday, and nobody had an appointment scheduled to view his horses until the weekend. Besides,

she didn't exactly seem as though she was in the market
to buy a horse.

"You sure don't look much like your football pictures."

Jackson narrowed his eyes. Had the paparazzi tracked
him down again? "People change after six years." He pulled
his hat lower on his forehead. His looks weren't the only
way he'd changed; his heart and lifestyle had both taken a
one-eighty. "Just who are you, anyway?"

"Uh—" the woman licked her pink lips "—I'm Mariah
Louisa Reyes."

Mariah Reyes. The name didn't ring any bells. Should
he know her? A memory invaded his mind—of a phone
call several weeks back. A memory of a reporter from the
Dallas Observer visiting the ranch so he could write an
article on Angelfire. Something Jackson had regretfully
allowed his brother, Evan, to cajole him into.

"Are you the reporter?" Hailey asked. "Uncle Evan said
you'd be coming."

What was that reporter's name? Rayburn—something.
Raymond? Reyes? The uneasy feeling in Jackson's belly
swirled faster than an Oklahoma tornado.

No!

"Yes," the woman said. "I work for the *Dallas Observer*. I'm supposed to stay here for a few days and ob-
serve how you gentle and train horses for rodeos for a
story I'm writing." She moved a step to the side, winced
and met Jackson's gaze, her black eyes shining like polished onyx. "People will be fascinated to learn how your
life has changed since you quarterbacked the Tornados,
Mr. Durant. The story will run in our Where Are They
Now? series."

"Oh, goodie," Hailey squealed, bouncing up and down,
clapping her hands together. "You're gonna be in the paper,
Daddy."

Great. Where Are They Now? series? Caution crept up

his spine. He'd worked hard to maintain his privacy the past years since moving to the ranch and didn't want strangers knowing where he lived. Besides, that article didn't sound like one that would promote the ranch—and that was his only reason for agreeing to it. Jackson cleared his throat. "You're the same reporter who talked to my brother, Evan Durant, and made arrangements to come here?"

The woman nodded.

He yanked off his hat and smacked it against his leg. "But I thought you were a man."

Ms. Reyes heaved a derisive snort. "Not hardly. Whatever gave you that idea?"

Where *had* he come up with it? Evidently he'd made a false assumption—or had his brother purposely led him in that direction, knowing he'd never allow a woman to stay at Angelfire? Evan was going to get a tongue-lashing. His brother knew he avoided women whenever possible, and he couldn't believe that Evan would make arrangements for one to stay at the ranch. Jackson never would have agreed to an interview if he'd known he'd be stuck with this prissy female.

He'd left the football high life and all its painful memories behind when he inherited the ranch from his uncle. And he certainly didn't want to spend even a few days in the company of a beautiful woman. The last time he did that, his life had turned upside down and inside out. He shut his eyes, refusing to think again of the woman he'd let into his life years earlier—the one who'd nearly destroyed him.

Curling the rim of his hat, he studied the dust on his boots. Dust this feisty female had stirred up. Somehow, Jackson had the feeling dirt wasn't the only thing this lovely, outspoken reporter would stir up. He just hoped she didn't dig up any dirt from his past. He preferred to keep that buried.

He smacked his hat against his leg again. His daughter

had nearly gotten killed. His filly had galloped off, and his dog had come close to getting run over. Better to end this now before it got any more out of hand. Jackson slapped his hat onto his head and glared at the reporter. "Ma'am, you can just head back to Dallas and forget about that interview."

TWO

Mariah couldn't voice the words that came to her mind with a child present. She'd finally drawn her first travel assignment, only to end up in the middle of Who-Knows-Where, Oklahoma, chased by a crazy person in a truck, with her beloved Mustang wrapped around a tree. And now this.

She narrowed her eyes and glared at J. D. Durant. She wasn't about to let this washed-up jock-turned-rancher chase her away or frustrate her any more than he already had. Moving slowly and testing each limb for pain, she ducked into the car. She pushed back the deflated air bag and sneezed again as the white powder danced in the air. Kneeling on the driver's seat, she reached across to the passenger's seat to grab her handbag. A sharp burning sensation exploded in her knee, sending pain throughout her leg. She sucked in a sharp gasp and backed out. As if sharing her hurt, the car door uttered an eerie, unnatural screech when she forced it shut.

Scowling at Jackson Durant, she limped to the rear of her car. With great effort, she willed the trembling in her hands to stop, pressed the button on the remote and popped open the trunk. At least the rear end of the car had avoided damage.

Hard footsteps marched toward her, sending her pulse

racing. J.D. hovered beside her, breathing loudly. A flash
of her father, doing the same right before he knocked her
silly, sent a shiver scurrying along her spine.

"What do you think you're doing?" His deep voice buzzed
her ears like an angry hornet. Steeling herself, Mariah ignored Mr. Durant and grabbed her largest bag. Giving it a
hard yank, she pulled it from the trunk then dropped it to the
ground. She turned around and reached in for her tote bag.

Sunshine entered her peripheral vision for a moment as
Mr. Durant bent and picked up her suitcase, then tossed it
back into the trunk.

"I said there isn't going to be an interview, so there's no
point in you staying."

Mariah straightened and, for the first time, realized what
an imposing figure Jackson Durant presented up close. His
photos didn't do him justice—or maybe the country life
agreed with him. With that dusty cowboy hat on his head
he had to be close to a foot taller than her. Eyes amazingly
similar to the dark blue of the Texas Tornados' football
uniform blazed at her, daring her to argue. An angular jaw
framed a handsome tanned face, and his pleasingly straight
nose looked out of place on an athlete. Dark brows that
matched thick hair the color of black coffee arched as she
continued to study him.

Rattled for a nanosecond, she regrouped and returned
his stare, leaning even closer. A victorious smile tugged
at the corners of her mouth. "Just how do you propose I
leave?"

His eyes flickered with confusion for a brief moment
then opened wider as understanding dawned. A muscle
quivered in his jaw. His lips tightened into a pale line, revealing a pair of intriguing dimples in his cheeks.

At least one good thing would come from her car being
almost totaled—she just might stay at Angelfire Ranch
long enough to get her story. It had been at least an hour's

drive since she'd passed a motel of any sort and much longer since seeing a decent one.

"I'm stranded," she said, not even trying to keep victory from her voice.

"She's right, Daddy." The young girl sidled up to her father and took his hand. "Her car's all smashed up, so she cain't leave."

"'Can't,' not 'cain't.'" Jackson smiled down at his daughter, but his lips slipped in a frown again as his gaze returned to Mariah.

What would it feel like to be on the receiving end of his heart-stopping smile? She'd seen plenty of them in the old photos she'd studied while researching him. She shook her head. Collecting smiles from an ex-superstar wasn't why she was here. She had a story to write.

He stared off in the distance, a muscle in his jaw twitching. His lips curled in resolve. "I'd offer to take you to town until your car's repaired, but there isn't a motel within sixty miles of here. I reckon you'll have to stay here while we see about getting it fixed. But no story." Arms crossed over his wide chest, he glared down at her, leaving no room for objection.

"Thanks for your…um…gracious offer." Her sarcasm prompted another scowl from him. Why did she do that? Rub salt in a wound. Maybe because as a child, she'd never been able to fight back. Maybe because she'd never had luck with men, especially confident, wealthy ones. Business execs always wanted something in return for a night on the town—something she was unwilling to give. Sports jocks were even worse. Arrogant. Cocky. So full of themselves there wasn't room for anyone else.

No, her track record with men wasn't good. Just standing this close to one gave her the shakes. She reached for her suitcase at the same instant he did, and his calloused hand enveloped hers, sending unwanted fingers of fire blazing up her arm. Mariah yanked her hand away.

"I'll get it," he mumbled, obviously not happy about losing their argument or her being stuck at his ranch. He turned and strode toward the house.

"C'mon. I'll show you where the spare room is," J.D.'s daughter said, skipping up to her. The girl grabbed the small bag. Mariah pushed her purse and laptop bag up on her shoulder then closed the trunk. Hailey took her by the arm and pulled her toward the sprawling ranch house. "I hope you can stay a long time. We don't ever have company stay overnight."

Mariah peeked at the child beside her. Where her dad was dark and brooding, his daughter was friendly and outgoing. Her hair was a much lighter shade of brown than his, and her eyes reminded Mariah of chocolate kisses.

Hailey slowed, leaned closer and whispered, "Daddy sure was surprised you're a woman. Uncle Evan must have forgot to tell him that." She peeked up at her father, who stood at the door holding the suitcase, then beamed a dimpled grin much like his.

"He's not the first to be shocked that I'm a female. The first was my father," Mariah said.

Hailey giggled. Mariah sensed that given the chance, she and the young girl could become friends. "So, how old are you?"

"Six."

"Six, huh?"

"Yep. I just had my birthday last week. Sometimes it's the same day as Thanksgiving, but not this year. I'll be seven next year."

A wave of melancholy washed over Mariah. Had she ever looked forward to a birthday? When she was a child, birthdays had been virtually nonexistent. Oh, they came and went like any other day, but they weren't celebrated, other than her mother slipping her a quarter, if she had one.

"Daddy says I can have my own horse when I'm older. He loves horses, but he loves football, too. Course, he don't play football no more. Well, 'cept sometimes he plays with Lance and Justin." Hailey skipped up the sidewalk that led to the cranberry-red front door of the gray brick ranch house.

Mariah filed the names Lance and Justin in a mental folder with plans to research them later, and then she studied the area. Though the house itself looked well kept, there was nothing special about the landscaping. In fact, the flower beds overflowed with dried grass and dead stalks. The only signs of life were a couple of dark green weeds and a few pitiful purple pansies that needed watering. The place sure could use a woman's touch.

Mariah's shoes scuffed against the sidewalk as she limped beside Hailey. Glancing down, she noticed a dark spot staining the knee of her new pantsuit, which was covered in white powder from the air bag. She quickly looked up before she got woozy. She must have banged her leg when she wrecked the car and was just now feeling the stinging sensation where the injury rubbed against her pants. She tried not to limp as she passed her reluctant host.

Hailey pulled open a screeching metal storm door, pushed against the main door and slipped inside. The screen slammed against Mariah's arm as she stepped across the threshold. The door handle scraped against her elbow, forcing her into the doorjamb. She winced.

"Sorry 'bout that," J.D. mumbled. He pulled back the door and held it while she walked in.

At least he had some manners.

Mariah looked around as her eyes adjusted to the dim light inside the house. They passed through a small mud-room and into a spacious kitchen decorated in dark green and yellow with wallpaper covered in birdhouses and tiny flowers. Everything was neat and tidy, not at all what she expected of a single father's home.

She followed Hailey, passing a more formal table and chairs in the dining room, which looked as if they were brand-new—a sign the family probably took their meals in the kitchen. Mariah peeked into the living area as they walked past the door, noting the Southwest theme with dark red, green and tan accents. Continuing down the hallway, they passed a closed door, and then Hailey walked into a bedroom with light blue walls.

"This is the guest bedroom. That's my room. It's painted lavender." She pointed to a closed door across the hall with a big purple-and-yellow daisy on it. "Daddy's is that way." Waving her hand in the air, she motioned on down the long hall.

Mariah glanced at J.D. and noticed his ears reddening, probably from the mention of his bedroom. She bit back a smile that such a tiny thing would rattle the rugged man after the way he lit into her for endangering his daughter. Ignoring the jealous ache caused by the thought of a father actually protecting his child, she turned her attention to the cozy bedroom. Powder-blue curtains matched the blue floral quilt on the queen-size bed. Through another door was a small bathroom that would give her privacy. She would be comfortable, even if she wasn't there for very long.

Her suitcase bounced as her host dropped it onto the bed. "I'll call Denton's shop in town and see if they can start repairing your car today." He turned and stalked out of the room, obviously anxious to be rid of her as soon as possible.

"Deuce says Daddy's kinda like a summer thunderstorm. He gets mad and blows up but calms down quickly."

Wondering who Deuce was, Mariah smiled at the young girl's analogy.

Hailey flopped onto the bed. "I'm glad you're a woman

even if Daddy isn't happy. Sometimes Aunt Kelly comes out and takes care of me, but not as much as she used to when I was little. She lived here then. This was her room."

The talkative child might be a wealth of information if Mariah could get to know her and could overcome her aversion to using the child to gain information on her father. She unzipped her suitcase, hoping for a longer stay than one night. "Where does your aunt Kelly live now?" She pulled out her black pantsuit, gave it a shake and hung it up in the empty closet.

"Oh, she lives in town. But she comes out here a lot." Hailey stopped her bouncing and leaned forward, a mischievous smile brightening her face. "She's sweet on Lance. At least she used to be."

"And who's Lance?"

"He owns the ranch next to us. He's Daddy's best friend."

"Hai—ley!" Jackson's bellow echoed down the hall. "Come and help Deuce put away the groceries."

Mariah smiled, certain he must have finally realized he'd left his chatty daughter alone with her.

"Okay!" Hailey took one last bounce and hopped off the bed.

"Who's Deuce?" Mariah asked as she hung a teal velour top on a hanger.

"Daddy's old friend. He lives here—in the room off the kitchen."

That was one room Mariah had obviously missed.

"He's really old. Daddy says he looks like he needs to be ironed, 'cause he gots so many wrinkles." Hailey giggled as she headed out the door. "Deuce is our cook."

Mariah wondered how old Hailey's version of "really old" was. The youth back at the Tank Up had called her "ma'am," even though she was only twenty-four.

She contemplated the black truck that had chased her as she arranged her folded clothing and undergarments in the empty dresser. Had the attack been random? Or maybe one of the cowboys from the bar just wanting to scare a city girl? What else could it have been? Not a soul in the state of Oklahoma knew her. She blew out a tense breath and set her suitcase in the bottom of the closet, next to her white tennis shoes. She sat on the chair that matched the small desk and looked at her pants. At least she hadn't torn her new business suit in the wreck, but she'd have to soak the pants in cold water to get the bloodstain out.

She rolled up her left pant leg, sucking in a deep breath as pain burned down her shin when she gently pulled the fabric away from an inch-long gash on her knee. A thin trail of blood ran halfway down her shin. Quickly, she shifted her gaze away.

Ignoring the nausea churning in her stomach, Mariah glanced around for a tissue. When she didn't find one, she dared to look more closely at her leg. The sight of blood had always made her feel like vomiting, if not fainting. She grabbed hold of the desk, desperately hoping the room would stop swirling. This was not the way to impress J. D. Durant and change his mind about the interview.

"Why didn't you tell me you were hurt?"

Mariah jumped at the closeness of J.D.'s masculine voice. No! Not now. Why did he have to appear just when she was at her weakest? She waved a dismissive hand in the air as she struggled to regain her composure.

Ignoring her, he disappeared into the bathroom and rummaged around for a minute, then returned with a bottle of hydrogen peroxide, ointment and bandages, which he set on the desk beside her. He returned to the bathroom, ran the faucet for a moment and came back with a damp cloth.

When he knelt beside her, Mariah sucked in a deep breath, mentally preparing herself for the task at hand. She reached for the aqua washcloth, but he pulled it away. "I can do it," she whispered, still not sure her stomach wasn't going to revolt and totally embarrass her.

He stoically ignored her again and gently cupped her calf, his warm touch sending odd tingles spiraling down her leg. She placed her hand on his shoulder, intending to push him away, but her gaze landed on the bloodstained cloth. Instantly she realized her mistake, but it was too late. Darkness swirled with light as she felt her body wilt.

Jackson dropped the wet washcloth and grabbed the reporter as she sagged toward him. Pushing to his feet, he lifted her in his arms and hugged her limp body against his chest. He couldn't believe this was the same spitfire who'd argued with him outside only minutes ago.

He laid her on the bed then pulled off her shoes. Snatching the clean washcloth off the floor, Jackson folded it in a long line and laid the clean side across her head. Now what? He'd never had a female faint on him before.

Was she injured worse than he first thought? There was the cut on her knee, but maybe she'd also banged her head in the accident and now had a concussion. Guilt plagued him for being so hard on her earlier. He may be a Christian, but he sure hadn't acted like one. He paced the room, trying to decide what he should do.

Why did women always cause him problems? This was the very reason he'd moved to the country, to get away from pesky, gawking fans and hovering women who wanted to be with him simply because he was a rich, famous athlete. He'd yielded to a woman's charms once, but that was a long time ago, and it wouldn't happen again.

"C'mon, Lord. Help me out here."

He could handle wounded horses and cows, could face a line of three-hundred-pound tacklers all bent on sacking him, but give him a sick or crying woman, and he lost all sensibility.

Get a grip, Durant.

A soft moan erupted from behind him, and he spun around. Ms. Reyes's arm rested across her forehead. He hurried to her side and eased onto the edge of the bed. "What can I do to help?"

She lifted the washcloth from her head, staring unseeing for a few moments. "Please…"

"What?" Jackson leaned forward, noticing her long, dark lashes.

"Please tell me I didn't pass out." She pressed her hand against her trim stomach.

"Wish I could, but—"

"Oh, I did, didn't I? I'm so embarrassed." A faint flush of scarlet darkened her olive skin, and then panic dashed across her pretty face as she scanned the room. "I didn't upset Hailey, did I?"

She started to sit up, but he gently grasped her shoulders, pressing her back down. Her concern for his daughter warmed him. Maybe he'd been too harsh and misjudged her at first glance. "You need to rest for a bit while I doctor your leg. And no, Hailey wasn't here when you passed out."

"Thank goodness. I wouldn't want to frighten her. She's such a sweet little thing."

"Yes, she is." Jackson smiled. Hailey could talk the ears off a mynah bird, but she certainly was a sweetie pie—and tough. She hadn't even fussed when Sabrina yanked her to the ground or when he'd doctored the rope burns on her hands a few minutes ago. He was proud of his daughter's fortitude, unlike this city gal, who fainted at the sight of a little gash. A ranch was no place for someone like her.

The sooner he patched up her leg, the sooner he could get away from her. He refocused his attention on the woman's injury and forced a politeness in his voice that he didn't feel. "If you're done with the washcloth, I'll finish cleaning your leg with it, Ms. Reyes."

Her cheeks darkened in a deep blush again. "Call me Mariah, and I can clean my own leg."

Jackson couldn't refrain from smirking. "I saw what happened when you merely looked at your bloody knee. How do you expect to stare at it long enough to doctor and bandage it? Am I wrong in guessing that you pass out at the sight of blood?"

Mariah's faced paled, and she glanced away. "No, you're not wrong," she said on a whisper. "This is so embarrassing. Go on and get it over with." She grabbed the damp cloth and tossed it in his direction.

He snagged it in midair, cleaned her wound, then washed off the blood that had trailed down her slim leg. "Are you hurt anywhere else?"

"No, not really, but I imagine I'll be sore tomorrow."

Relief washed over him as he cleansed the wound with peroxide. He squeezed some triple antibiotic salve onto the inch-long gash then applied two wide bandages. No problem. Just like treating one of Hailey's banged-up knees. Well, not exactly, but at least the woman didn't cry or fuss about it hurting. Without thinking, Jackson reached behind Mariah's leg and gave her calf a soft caress, just like he would Hailey's. He wasn't prepared for the electric arc that sprinted up his arm. He released her as if he'd been shocked and glanced up.

His eyes locked with her black gaze and held. Awareness sizzled between them.

"Daddy, I'm done helpin' Deuce." Hailey peered in the doorway. "Are you gonna go catch Sabrina? Can I go, too?"

Instantly his connection with the troublesome reporter severed. He shook his head, unable to comprehend what had just happened. Leaping off the bed, he accidentally looked in Mariah's direction again.

She must have sensed whatever it was he had felt, because she wore a dazed expression, too—or maybe she'd gotten a glimpse of the bloody washrag. Jackson shrugged off the unwanted sensations. This wasn't good.

Women were trouble, and he had enough trouble already—especially with all the strange goings-on lately. To make matters worse, Tim Denton couldn't begin fixing the reporter's car until the first of next week—and that was if the vehicle wasn't totaled. He was stuck with the nosy reporter for at least the whole weekend since Westin, the nearest town to the ranch, didn't have a motel—or a car rental agency.

"Oh, you hurt your leg?" Hailey crossed the room to the bed, and Jackson stepped back.

"It's nothing. Just a little cut." Mariah sat up and rolled down her pant leg then turned to sit on the side of the bed. "Your dad patched me up."

"He's good at fixin' things. See, he put princess bandages on my hands."

Hailey held up her palms as if they were trophies and flashed him a dimpled smile, sending a warm sensation, better than a cup of hot coffee on a chilly day, down his midsection.

"So, what about Sabrina?"

"I'll catch her." He stalked out, not bothering to look at the reporter again. He and his daughter were a team. They got along fine and didn't need another female around to mess up things. He especially didn't need a reporter around when problems were plaguing him. What if she got hurt? Or what if she told the world about what had been happening here?

He clenched his jaw. He needed to get her car fixed and get her on the road home.

THREE

Delicious odors wafting from the kitchen lured Mariah out of her room and down the hallway. The door near the living room that had previously been closed was now open. Her reporter's instinct and insatiable curiosity drew her to the unknown, and she couldn't resist a peek.

Stepping inside the room, her gaze immediately focused on a huge desk positioned in front of a large picture window that offered a tranquil view of a small pond and a pasture with grazing horses. In the distance, on the far side of the pasture, a car zipped by on the same road she'd recently traveled, snagging her attention. Her pulse kicked up several notches as her thoughts veered to the black truck again. Should she have mentioned it to Jackson? If she hadn't made that turn on time she could have been killed. No, it was probably nothing. Just some country boys having fun at her expense. At least that was what she wanted to believe. She shook away the troubling image and continued to look around the room.

Along the far wall was a wide oak credenza with a computer and printer. Papers littered the adjacent desk in what she felt sure was some kind of chaotic order. The walls were covered in pictures of horses, eagles and football memorabilia.

Jackson's office. He probably spent his evenings working at the desk or reading in the hunter-green leather recliner. A well-worn leather Bible lay on top of a pile of magazines on an end table next to the chair. While the rest of the house was neat and orderly, this room looked as if a housekeeper hadn't touched it in a decade.

Curiosity sated for the moment, she backed out and headed toward the sound of voices coming from the kitchen, if she wasn't mistaken. Her mouth watered at the fragrant scent of frying chicken. She rounded the corner and stopped. Hailey stood on a step stool, washing potatoes in the sink beside a grizzled old man who was dicing tomatoes and adding them to a salad.

He glanced over his shoulder and flashed a whiskery, gap-toothed smile. "You must be that reporter I heard so much about. Kind of got J.D. all stirred up in a tizzy, what with you bein' a woman and all."

She cringed inwardly at his remark but struggled to keep her discomfort from reflecting in her expression. Just what had Mr. Durant said about her?

The old man deftly chopped two stalks of green onions and slid the pieces off the cutting board into the salad. Using a long-handled spoon and fork, he stirred the mixture then shoved it into the refrigerator. He closed the fridge door and grinned. "I'm Deuce, J.D. and Hailey's chief cook and bottle washer."

Giggling, Hailey peeked over her shoulder, eyes twinkling. "You don't wash bottles. We put them in the dishwasher."

Mariah and Deuce exchanged a knowing smile. She studied the man from his mad-professor hairdo to his baggy, faded blue overalls and scuffed cowboy boots. A cook was the last thing she'd expect this strange character to be. Still, he'd seemed quite handy at mixing his salad. He stabbed a flour-coated drumstick in a skillet and deftly flipped it over, revealing its golden side. The chicken popped and sizzled, filling the room with a tantalizing aroma. She'd never seen anyone fry chicken before, and she watched, mesmerized.

The door to the mudroom opened and a tall, handsome man strode through it and into the kitchen as though he owned the place. He aimed for the stove and failed to notice her standing just outside the kitchen. He lifted his nose in the air. "Mmm…fried chicken. Deuce, you seen J.D.? And whose smashed-up Mustang is that?"

The stranger was several inches shorter than Jackson, but with his stout build, long blond hair and crystal-blue eyes, he resembled an ancient Viking warrior—at least he would if not for his Western hat and clothing. He turned in her direction and his brows lifted as she moved into the room, keeping the table between them. Mariah felt a flicker of familiarity and sorted through her mental files but still couldn't place him.

His lips turned up in a welcoming grin. "Well, now, this is a surprise. I never expected to encounter a lovely female at ol' J.D.'s house. Thought maybe he was allergic to them. *Hola, señorita.*" The man tipped his Western hat as Deuce chuckled.

She stared back and gave a curt nod, choosing to ignore his ethnic greeting. Mariah gripped the top of the chair in front of her and considered his reaction to her being at the ranch. Why would a handsome, robust man like J.D. not want women around? Had that pain of losing his wife been so much that he'd sworn off women?

"Females are girls, and I'm a girl, Lance." Hailey dropped her peeled potato into a bowl of water, sloshing it all over the counter. "Daddy's not 'lergic to me. What's *'lergic,* anyway?"

"Nothin', munchkin," Deuce said. "Go find your pa and tell him Lance is here to see 'im. I'll finish the spuds." He passed the girl a towel to dry her hands.

Hailey swiped her palms, tossed the towel on the counter

and ran through the mudroom and out the door, obviously happy to be free of kitchen duty.

"I'm Lance Jordan, J.D.'s nearest neighbor and an old friend. I own the ranch just down the road a ways." He stuck out his tanned, calloused hand.

She leaned closer, glad for the table that separated them, and shook it. "Mariah Reyes." That tiny flicker of remembrance sparked again, and this time, it flamed to life. Of course. Lance Jordan. He was on the Tornado team the same time Jackson was. In fact, he stayed on the team until an accident early this season sidelined him.

He winked at her, and Mariah removed her hand. Some females might be attracted to his cocky attitude, but she much preferred a kind, humble man. One thing was certain: Lance's megawatt smile would make most single women do a double take.

"So, what brings you to our neck of the woods? J.D. didn't mention that a pretty gal was due to pay him a visit, but then, I can see why he'd like to keep that news a secret." He wagged his pale brows and smirked. "Doesn't care much for competition now that he's retired from football."

She shrugged and was tempted to return to her room, but then a thought blossomed. A friend of Jackson's might be an excellent source of information. She smiled. "I'm here to do a story for the *Dallas Observer*'s Where Are They Now? column."

Whistling through his teeth, Lance glanced at Deuce. The old man grinned and lifted one shoulder as he cut up the potatoes. "I don't believe this." Lance leaned against the counter and shifted his gaze back to her. "J.D.'s always so private. He hates publicity. How'd you ever talk him into it?"

Before she could tell him the interview had been arranged by her boss, Deuce piped up, "She didn't. Evan cooked up the whole thing and somehow got Jackson to go along with it. Somethin' about Angelfire needin' publicity." The old man dumped the potato cubes into a pot of boiling water and surveyed his chicken.

Lance's baffled expression must have mirrored her own. Mariah wondered how J. D. Durant, famous football personality and former media hound, had turned into a recluse who passionately guarded his privacy better than a quarterback protected a football. She figured it had something to do with his daughter.

Lance shook his head. "I can't believe J.D. let his geeky brother talk him into having a reporter do a story on him. Especially a female reporter—and with everything that's been happening around here."

Mariah stiffened. In the newspaper field, she constantly battled prejudiced male attitudes, but she wasn't about to retreat. Then she realized what else he'd said. "What's been happening?"

Deuce let out a strange cackle, ignoring her question. "Well, now, that there's the funny part. Evan forgot to mention that fact. Seems our boy never once considered the reporter might be female, and by the time he found out the truth, she was already stuck here—at least until her car's fixed. That mangled heap you asked about is hers."

Lance's dazed expression lasted only a moment. His gaze sparked, and he bent over hooting with laughter. He smacked his thigh three times, and then he rubbed his hand over his moist eyes. "That's great!"

"What's great?" Jackson walked through the mudroom and into the kitchen, glancing around, obviously wondering what he'd missed.

Lance instantly sobered. "Uh…nothing. Just something funny Deuce said."

When Jackson's blue gaze turned her way, Mariah blew out a frustrated breath, knowing her question wouldn't be answered now that Jackson had returned. Something seemed to be going on here at Angelfire, besides ranching—and she had to find out what. Maybe her story would take a turn she hadn't expected.

Jackson pursed his lips. He'd hoped to keep his visitor's presence a secret until he could send her on her way. No chance of that now that Lance had seen her. "I guess you all have met."

Lance grinned. "'Bout time you came out of hiding. I'm gonna have to get this pretty gal alone and tell her all your secrets."

Jackson's stomach churned. Was Lance teasing? Sometimes he was hard to read. His friend loved being the center of attention and broadcasting any news he was privileged to. With Lance around, the small town of Westin hardly needed a weekly newspaper. Jackson sighed. He'd have to do what he could to keep Lance and Ms. Reyes apart. "So, what brings you here this time of day, Lance?"

"Thought you'd want to know your horses got out."

"Horses?" He'd put Sabrina back in her stall and had left Hailey down there talking to the filly while he came up to the house to fetch some salve to put on a scrape on the horse's leg.

"Mmm-huh," Lance said, without taking his eyes off the reporter.

Jackson could smell trouble brewing. With Ms. Reyes here for close to a week, it would be nigh impossible to keep Lance away from her. He walked to the fridge and pulled out a bottle of water to quench his mega thirst. Watching him, Mariah licked her lips, and he realized he wasn't being much of a host. He held the chilled bottle out to her, pleased when her eyes sparked with surprise. She gave him an impish grin then walked over and took the container. He didn't bother offering one to Lance. He'd help himself if he was thirsty. And by the way Lance stared at Ms. Reyes, Jackson guessed he wasn't thirsty but hungry—woman hungry.

He cleared his throat, drawing Lance's gaze. "I just caught that filly. She got loose and ran down the drive earlier. Found her munching grass on County Line Road." Jackson took a swig of water to avoid mentioning how the filly had gotten loose. Mariah glanced at him, offering a diminutive smile, probably thanking him for not embarrassing her with the truth.

"So what happened to that Mustang out there? That tree up and ambush it?" Lance chuckled, helping himself to a piece of lettuce lying on the counter.

A red-wine color stained Mariah's cheeks as she sipped her water with the grace of royalty. Her gaze locked with Jackson's for a moment, and then she quietly studied the floor tiles.

"Well, we, uh—had a little accident. The filly got spooked and ran in front of Ms. Reyes's car, and she had to swerve to miss her."

Mariah's tense expression relaxed. Jackson sucked in a deep breath as a surge of chivalry warmed his chest.

"Guess you're stuck here for a while," Lance said. "Especially since Tim Denton's out of town until Saturday, and he's closed on the weekends. But, hey, just let me know if you need a ride somewhere."

Great! Jackson lobbed the empty water bottle in the recycle tub that sat to the left of the fridge. Leave it to Lance to spill the beans.

Mariah's questioning gaze touched his face. "Who's Tim Denton?" she asked, twisting her bottle in her hands.

"He's the only guy in these parts that works on cars." An ornery smile tilted Lance's mouth. "So it looks like you're going to have to make yourself at home here for a while—unless, of course, you'd rather have some classy company and want to come stay with me." Lance pulled a toothpick from his shirt pocket and stuck it in his mouth.

Jackson didn't miss the victorious expression that flashed across Ms. Reyes's face for a brief moment. Was it because she thought she'd get to stay long enough to get her story? Or because she was interested in Lance's offer? Jackson winced. He would prefer to have her out from under his boot heels, but there was no way he'd allow Lance to take her home. He might not want her staying at Angelfire, but he sure wouldn't throw her into the wolf's den.

"She'll be fine here. Hailey's taken a likin' to her." He forced the words out, finally accepting that Mariah Reyes would be around for the time being.

Surprise flickered in her dark eyes again, and then a pleasant smile graced her lips. Jackson stared out the window, not caring for the way his insides reacted to her.

Deuce pulled some dishes out of the cabinet and clunked them down on the counter. "You stayin' for supper?" he asked Lance.

"Nah. I'd like to, but I've got a date. Just came down to let J.D. know about his horses getting loose. Looks like they broke through that section of fence down by the creek."

Jackson blinked. Horses? As in plural? "You mean more than one got loose? I thought you were talking about Sabrina, the filly that got spooked."

Lance straightened from leaning against the counter. "I wondered why you didn't seem too worried. Yeah, there was six or seven of 'em across the road, grazing near old lady Murphy's garden. If they get in her flower bed, you'll never hear the end of it, even if everything is dead now."

Jackson yanked his hat off and smacked it against his leg. He didn't need another problem. This was the third time in two weeks his horses had gotten out—and they'd never broken out before. Something didn't sit right. He was beginning to think someone had it in for him. This week he'd discovered that one of his stock tanks had been used for target practice, and last week, several head of cattle had gone missing and hadn't been found yet.

He curled the brim of his hat with his hands. Were the incidents the work of bored teenagers? Or was someone deliberately doing damage to his ranch?

But why would anyone do that? He had no enemies—at least none that he knew of.

Slapping his hat back on, he looked at Lance. "You got time to help me round up those strays?"

"Thought you'd never ask. Just need to hurry." Lance grinned. "Can't be late for my date, you know."

"Let's do it, then, and maybe I can get back in time to eat my dinner while it's still warm."

Mariah walked toward him with a concerned look in her eyes. "Is there…uh…anything I can do?"

He shook his head. Just what he needed—for this citified greenhorn to get injured again. He would probably have to pay to get her car repaired, not to mention possibly being hit with a hefty lawsuit. "Stay put."

Mariah flinched at the tone of his voice and looked at the floor. Jackson winced. Maybe she really did want to help and not just get a story. He could at least protect her without being a bully. "Maybe you could keep Hailey busy so she doesn't run outside when we herd the horses up the drive."

She nodded. A smile brightened her face, and Jackson got a peek at how pretty Mariah Reyes really was. Straight black hair framed her face with feminine grace. Onyx eyes danced and her white teeth stood out against her chestnut skin.

He shook his head. *Don't even go there, Durant. This woman is trouble wrapped up in a pretty package.*

"You said Hailey was still outside?" Mariah asked.

"She's in the barn, talking to Sabrina."

Mariah nodded, looking eager to leave the male-dominated room. "I'll walk out and let her know supper is about ready."

As Jackson opened the door for her, a high-pitched scream jerked his head toward the barn. *Hailey!*

Jackson raced to the barn. His daughter was tough, not one given to hysterics, but that scream had been frantic. Baron's frenzied barking added to his concern. His gut forced him to skid to a halt just inside the barn door to survey the situation. As his eyes rapidly searched the dimmer interior, he found his daughter clinging to the hayloft ladder, several rungs off the ground. Footsteps pounded behind him, and a quick glance told him Lance, Deuce and the reporter had followed him. "Baron! Quiet." The dog trotted to his side, looked up and whined.

"Daddy!"

Relief swarmed him at the sound of his daughter's voice. He started toward her. The horses in the stalls closest to him snorted and pranced in their small enclosures, sending a shiver of warning down his spine. He scanned the back of the barn, searching for the problem. With all that had been going on lately, he couldn't afford to drop his guard—but that was just what had happened since that reporter had distracted him. He started toward Hailey. "What's wrong, precious?"

"No! Stop! There's a snake." She pointed to her left, waving her hand up and down.

Jackson blew out a pent-up breath, the tension rolling off him. "Since when have you been afraid of—" The eerie clatter of a rattlesnake's tail yanked his attention to the gate of the nearest stall. Lightning whinnied and reared, his hooves pounding hard against the gate. The snake swiveled its head toward the horse and away from Jackson's daughter.

"A diamondback? Where in the world did that come from?" Lance moved up on Jackson's right.

"Stay on the ladder, Hailey. Do not come down until I say so."

She nodded and looped her arm around a rung.

"I'll get a shovel." Lance started toward the far wall, but after he passed by, Jackson moved to the left side of the barn door and reached up on a high shelf. He pulled down a pistol he'd kept there for an emergency—like this one. He moved several feet closer then aimed and fired. The snake lurched then settled in death.

He put the safety on the gun and rushed to his daughter, scooping her into his arms. What if the snake had bitten her before she'd noticed it? *Thank You, Lord, for protecting her.*

"Where did that thing come from?" Ms. Reyes asked. "I didn't think rattlesnakes were common this far north, and they aren't usually active this late in the year."

Jackson shook his head and hugged Hailey. "I don't know. It's the first I've seen on the ranch. Most of the snakes we have here are harmless, except for water moccasins." He shuddered, again thinking what might have happened.

Lance trotted over with his shovel. "I didn't know you kept a gun out here."

Hailey wiggled, and Jackson set her down. "Good thing I do."

Hailey walked closer to the dead snake and stared at it. "I've never seen a snake so big. That rattle thing on its tail is cool."

Lance stepped between the child and the snake. "Don't get too close, short stuff. That snake still has deadly venom in its fangs." He looked over his shoulder at Jackson. "I'll bury it if you want to get her up to the house."

"I can take her—since you still need to catch those horses." Mariah gazed at Jackson with her eyebrows lifted.

"My chicken!" Deuce spun around and took off running like a calf let out of a rodeo chute.

Lance chuckled.

Jackson nodded. "Hailey, go on back to the house with Ms. Reyes."

"But I was giving Sabrina some hay."

"Go on. I'll finish up."

"Okay." She jogged over to their guest and took her hand. "Wanna see my princess dolls?"

"Uh, sure." Ms. Reyes allowed herself to be dragged across the clearing to the house.

Lance sidled up to him. "That reporter sure took me by surprise. Pretty thang, isn't she?"

Jackson glanced sideways. "She's off-limits, and she's leaving the minute her car is fixed."

"Whoa, cowboy." Lance held up a hand.

"I need to catch my horses. Go ahead and take care of that snake. Bury it deep so Baron won't dig it up—or better yet, burn it somewhere and then come and help me herd the horses home."

Lance nodded and scooped the snake onto the shovel. Jackson headed into the room where he stored his motorcycle, both thankful for how God had protected Hailey from the snake and irritated somewhat at Lance. His friend always saw a pretty woman as a challenge to conquer. He hoped Lance didn't give the reporter trouble—or tell any of the many secrets he knew about Jackson's former life. A life he'd just as soon forget.

He opened the side door to the garage, hopped on his motorcycle and shoved on his helmet, then started the bike. The loud sound of the powerful engine revving up mirrored his mood. He steered the bike outside and down the drive.

Where had that snake come from? Jackson had no doubt someone had planted it in his barn. But why? He shuddered to think Hailey had been out there all alone. What if she'd gone to visit Lightning after feeding Sabrina? What if the filly had heard the snake and spooked when Hailey was in her stall? She could have been badly injured, at the least. A cold chill settled in his chest. Someone was out to get him—and didn't care if they hurt his daughter in the process.

He looked around for signs of someone watching him as he pulled onto the main road but saw no one. It was clear now that teens couldn't be the source of his problems. Someone wanted to hurt him, and he had no idea who it was or why. The picture of his daughter on that ladder just a few yards from a deadly snake made his gut swirl. He'd have to keep a better watch on Hailey—and the reporter—until things settled down. But when would that be?

Who could hate him so much that they'd risk killing his daughter?

With both hands clasping her warm mug, Mariah sat at the kitchen table, sipping her morning coffee. After a quick breakfast, Jackson and Hailey had made a mad dash out the door to the entrance of the ranch to meet a neighbor who would take Hailey to school. Deuce had disappeared into his room for his morning devotions, muttering they needed all the prayers they could get.

Mariah hoped she hadn't offended him when she'd refused to eat seconds. As delicious as the bacon and eggs with homemade biscuits and gravy were, she couldn't have eaten another bite. If she ate like that every meal, she'd probably gain ten pounds before she went home.

She studied Hailey's childish drawings stuck on the refrigerator door with magnets and smiled. Contentment drifted around her like a fresh snowfall. This house felt peaceful. Like a real home—something she'd never really had. Oh, growing up she'd had a place to live, if you could call that dilapidated trailer livable, but it wasn't homey like this place.

This family truly loved and supported one another. Jackson's affection for his daughter was evident with his twinkle-eyed smiles, bear hugs and quick kisses to the top of her head. He couldn't seem to keep his eyes off Hailey last night. Had he been thinking how close he'd come to losing her?

As Mariah had lain in bed last night, she'd pondered the snake incident and why someone would have put it in the barn—she had no doubts someone had. Rattlesnakes weren't active this far north in December, so it meant someone had kept it in a warm environment until it was needed. Had they hoped to kill Jackson—or did they not care who they hurt? Could the incident be connected to the horses getting loose?

She had found nothing on the internet about Jackson that would warrant someone wishing him dead. What a loss it would be to Hailey to lose her loving father after growing up without her mother. Mariah stared into her coffee cup. She'd never known a father's affection—could barely even imagine what it must be like to have a man love and protect her. Her father had never been affectionate or caring. The only thing she could ever remember him hugging was his liquor bottle, and because of his drunken state, she'd been forced to wait on him and her brother constantly, even as a young child.

By the time she was twelve, her mother was so beaten down and frail that a simple cold turned into pneumonia. Mariah grasped the warm cup. She didn't want to remember those awful days before her mama died, but the memories gushed back. Her father had said they couldn't afford to take Mama to the hospital, but if they had she might have lived. Looking back on the situation now, Mariah wondered if her father had refused to allow Mama to go because he knew the doctor would have found signs of abuse. As she cared for her mother, she'd seen the angry bruises and welts her clothing normally hid. Tears dampened Mariah's eyes, and her breathing deepened. Her father was a coward—a man who hit his wife and his daughter.

The day her mama died, she became the maid—or rather,

the slave. Cooking and cleaning. Washing the clothes. Even doing the grocery shopping, all while trying to keep her grades at school at a passing level. She pushed away the morose memories and glanced at the remaining biscuits sitting on a plate in the middle of the table. Why could a wrinkled old man make golden, flaky ones from scratch while she burned the kind that came from a can?

"Why so serious?"

Mariah jumped, sloshing coffee onto her fingers. Wincing, she set the mug down, grabbed a napkin from the holder in the center of the table and wiped off the hot liquid. She'd been so deep in thought she hadn't even heard Jackson return.

"Guess you got Hailey off to school?" As a reporter, she was an expert at deflecting conversation.

"Yeah." A gentle smile tilted his lips. "But I had a hard time. She wanted to stay home because you were here—and honestly, I almost caved after what happened last night. But I made her go. I told her you'd be here several days. Plus, I reminded her that tomorrow is Saturday."

Mariah sipped what was left of her coffee and watched over the top of her mug as Jackson unsnapped his denim jacket and hung it and his hat on hooks in the mudroom. He dressed like she imagined a typical rancher did, in a blue plaid flannel shirt and jeans. The chair across from hers squeaked as he lowered his big body onto it. Steam spiraled upward from the cup of coffee he poured from the stainless-steel carafe. He lifted the pitcher in her direction, and she slid her cup forward, letting him refill it, and then he set the carafe on the side of the table and picked up his cup. As he sipped his brew, his gaze captured hers.

Goose bumps charged up her arms. She'd never had breakfast and morning coffee in a man's home before, especially not with a guy this good-looking. There was something satisfying about it, and the fact that she wasn't shaking in her boots at being alone with him gave her hope that someday she might be comfortable in a relationship with a man. Could it be someone like Jackson Durant?

No. She dropped her gaze to study the tablecloth's plaid pattern. Her brother had been a football player, basking in the adoration of the female fans at their high school. It had turned her stomach. She knew well that kind of man could also turn his physical prowess into a weapon if he chose to. She had a few scars to prove it.

"What's going on in that pretty head of yours?"

Mariah glanced up, surprised that he'd called her "pretty." Instantly, Jackson's dark blue gaze captured hers. He had beautiful eyes—like a summer's sky at twilight. Not pale blue like Lance Jordan's but more like dazzling sapphires. And those long, black lashes. Why did Mother Nature give men lashes like that while women had to apply layers of mascara to achieve the same effect?

"You're awfully quiet. Guess you're not a morning person." Jackson sipped his coffee then reached for a biscuit.

"Sorry. I've been doing a lot of thinking."

"Worried about your car?"

Her car? She probably should be thinking about the vehicle, but it hadn't even entered her mind. She needed to call her insurance company and also let her boss know she wouldn't be back on Monday. "I hope I didn't kill your tree. Will you tell me next spring? I can replace it if I did."

Jackson looked surprised by her offer but waved a dismissive hand in the air. "It's just a tree. Don't worry about it."

"But it's my fault."

"No, you're right that the filly ran in front of you. That's partly my fault because I let Hailey walk her around."

He stared at her while he munched another biscuit. Mariah could see the wheels turning in his mind—probably contemplating how she'd been driving too fast or how he wasn't prepared for her to be a woman. She wondered why his brother had kept that bit of information from him. Brothers had a way of messing things up. At least, hers sure had.

"How's your knee today?"

"Better. A bit sore, but I'll live."

"You, uh, think you might feel up to taking a tour of the ranch?"

Her heart jolted as hope soared. Had he changed his mind about the interview?

He held up his palm. "Now don't get ahead of me. I didn't say anything about doing the interview. It's just that…" He pursed his lips and stared out the window for a long moment then faced her again. "I could use a fresh set of eyes. I've had some strange things happening lately and can't decide if they are a coincidence or if someone's out to get me."

Mariah straightened in her chair, sniffing the makings of a real story. "You mean like a snake in the barn?" She wished she had her digital tablet to make notes on, but then, Jackson would probably clamp his mouth shut if he caught her using it.

"Yeah." Resting his elbow on the table, he plowed his fingers through his hair then leaned his head against his hand. "I don't know. I thought I was just being a worrywart until last night's event. I've had fences cut and horses get out onto the road several times in the past few weeks. Yesterday, six got out. I found five of them, but one's still missing. Course, it's possible she's just hiding out somewhere on the ranch. She's due to foal soon. She may have wandered off to give birth."

"That doesn't sound so bad. At least you caught all but the one."

"Yeah, but there are no lights on the county roads at night. Someone could have run into one of the horses while they were out and damaged their car or gotten hurt, not to mention injuring the horse."

"Do you think it could be teenagers?"

He shrugged. "I honestly don't know."

"Got any enemies? Unhappy customers?"

"No, not really."

"What about competitors for horse sales?"

"I did recently sign a contract to supply the Oklahoma Rodeo Federation with horses and some bulls, but I don't know anyone who'd go to such extremes to keep me from selling a few dozen horses, though. All the folks I know around here are good, solid folk. They help their neighbors, not destroy their property."

"It's not that way where I come from." She pushed away that troubling thought and tapped her fingers on the table, wondering if now was a good time to mention the black-truck incident. Maybe it was somehow connected. "There's something I probably should tell you."

His eyebrows lifted. "What's that?"

She stared out the window, took a breath and told him about stopping at the Tank Up and the black trucks that followed her. "I don't know what might have happened if I hadn't reached your drive just when I did. That truck was closing in on me."

"Why would anyone chase you? Nobody here knows you."

She shrugged. "I wondered the same thing. But hearing about your troubles, I can't help wondering if they might be related."

Jackson rubbed his nape. "I doubt it. My problems started before you arrived."

"How long ago?"

"A couple of weeks, I reckon."

"And you don't remember anything that happened before that to cause someone to be upset with you?"

He shook his head. "Everybody in these parts is friendly, and most seem proud to have an ex–pro ball player—two actually—as neighbors. Some have even helped steer strangers away when they've asked for directions to Angelfire."

Mariah smiled. "No wonder it's so hard to find this place."

"I like my privacy." He grinned but then sobered. "It keeps my daughter safe—at least it has until yesterday."

She straightened. "You don't think someone's out to hurt Hailey, do you?"

"No. There's no reason to believe that."

Mariah wrapped her palms around her coffee mug. "What about the rattlesnake? My gut says someone planted it in the barn."

His sober gaze captured hers. "I wondered that, too. Someone would have to hate me an awful lot to risk killing one of us—and that's what would have happened if that diamondback had bitten anyone."

"You've lived in the real world before—the cutthroat world where people find it easier to take what they want than work hard. It makes more sense that snake was planted than it just happened to show up, especially with it being almost winter."

"It's true that I used to bask in the limelight, but it's different here. These people are different. Most are good churchgoing folk." Jackson lurched from his chair and paced the room. "I can't believe anyone I know would risk hurting my daughter. There has to be another explanation."

"Just because someone attends church, it doesn't make them a saint." She stood and walked over to where he stared out the window. "So, if it's not someone from around here causing your problems, who else could it be? Someone from your past?"

He was silent for a long moment then blew out a loud sigh. "I have no idea."

She hated seeing the vulnerability in this big, rugged man. She laid her hand on his forearm. "I'll do whatever I can to help you figure out what's going on."

"I appreciate that." He nodded and looked down. "But don't think I'll change my mind about the story."

She tightened her jaw and stepped back. So much for bridging the gap between them. "I understand, but you must also understand that I have a job to do."

He spun away from the window. "I need to fix that fence. We can take the tour I mentioned while we're out there."

"We?"

"You want to see the ranch, don't you?"

Maybe she could learn something about him while he was showing her his ranch. She certainly wouldn't if she stayed here and let him go alone. Mariah nodded.

He stared at her for a long moment then quirked his intriguing mouth to one side. "You got anything to wear besides those fancy city duds?"

She looked at her velour top and knit pants. Fancy city duds? These were her lying-around-don't-have-to-work-today clothes. Her comfy clothes.

"You got any jeans? Don't suppose you have a pair of boots?" His gaze looked hopeful.

"Jeans, yes. Boots, no."

"Well, go change, and I'll meet you at the barn. I need to pack some supplies."

Back in her room, Mariah let her laptop warm up while she donned her jeans and a flannel shirt that she'd tossed in her suitcase at the last moment. She kicked off her slippers then sat at the desk and started typing.

Jackson Durant—bossy, can be rude, protective of his daughter, obsessive about his privacy. Handsome—amazing dimples when he smiles...

Mariah blew out a breath, hit the return key and began typing again.

Hailey—Jackson's daughter. Cute, sweet, precocious (must take after her mother).

Lance Jordan—friend, neighbor, played football with Jackson. Cocky. Arrogant.

Deuce—cook, Jackson's old friend.

Justin?

Kelly—Jackson's younger sister.

Evan Durant—Jackson's brother. Bad feelings between the two?

Well, it wasn't much to start with, but it was a beginning. After touring the ranch today, surely she'd have more information for her article. She reached up to close her laptop but paused, and then she added:

Problems on ranch:

Rattlesnake in barn.

Horses getting out of fences.

Cattle missing.

Shot-up stock tanks.

Accidents or sabotage?

On a whim, she added: Black truck chasing cars.

One way or another, she had to get Jackson to agree to let her do her story. Maybe if she could help him with his problem, he might be more willing to grant the interview.

Considering yesterday's events, Jackson reached onto the shelf for his gun—the one he'd shot the rattler with—thinking it would be best to stay armed until things settled down. But as he groped along the back of the shelf, he couldn't find the weapon. He shoved his hands to his hips and looked around the barn. Things had been a bit chaotic, but hadn't he returned it after making sure Hailey was unhurt? Or had he taken it inside?

Glancing at his watch, he shook his head. How long did it take for that woman to change clothes?

He blew out a breath, thinking how pretty Mariah had looked, nibbling on her lip as she contemplated the problems he was having. And he had to admit it was nice to have someone to discuss them with—and to share coffee with. Mariah was a beautiful woman, and those dark eyes of hers seemed to reach into the abyss of his lonely soul. He was starting to like her—a lot.

Jackson growled, frustrated with his train of thought. He wished he'd never agreed to let Evan arrange the interview. He'd only done it to help promote the ranch and to get his brother off his back. The fact that Evan hadn't mentioned Ms. Reyes was a female reporter still rankled him. The truth of the matter was, he didn't want anyone— male or female—invading his privacy. He'd done his time and paid his dues to the public when he'd played football. Now he simply wanted a quiet life for him and his daughter.

As he searched the tack room and several more places where he might have put the gun, his mind drifted back to earlier days. Never once had he regretted walking away from football. Yeah, he missed the game that had been his complete focus from the time he started playing in elementary school. He'd loved the success and attention it had brought him. But that was then.

He no longer needed swarming fans, people vying for his autograph or sexy cheerleaders begging for his attention to make him feel important. He had God now. Faith had filled a hole that he'd once crammed full with public adoration, success as a football player and the love of a beautiful woman.

A cold chill galloped down his spine whenever he thought of Misty—the beautiful betrayer.

"Now who's the serious one?"

"What?" Jackson jerked his head up to see Mariah standing in the barn's entrance.

"You look like you're in another world."

He had been in another world. One he'd prefer to forget, if not for Hailey. Jackson walked toward the woman in front of him. The citified gal had been replaced by one who looked more like a country girl, but the newness of her clothes and those spotless white sneakers gave her away. Dark blue denim jeans clung to her slim legs like new paint on a barn, and her blue flannel shirt looked as soft as a horse's muzzle. Her lavender jacket hung open and would look more at home on a ski slope than a ranch. And those shoes. One thing for sure, they wouldn't be bright white for long. He bit back a smile at the familiar green stain along the sole of one shoe. Wouldn't this city gal just die if she knew what she was standing in?

Jackson spun around to hide the grin that cracked his face. "Come on in. The horses don't bite. Well, most of them don't."

He got his snicker under control and turned around. The reporter still stood at the barn door, looking scared half to death. Her gaze darted from stall to stall then up to the hayloft as she took in everything.

She was probably a good reporter. Nothing seemed to get past her, and she asked a wheelbarrow full of questions. But...

"I'm not getting on one of those." The whites of her eyes showed, and she wouldn't cross the barn's threshold.

Jackson shook his head. How did she ever manage to get assigned to do a ranch story?

"I can help you mount," he said. "That's no big deal."

"Th-they're too big." She retreated several steps.

"Here, put this on."

She stared at him, and her pretty mouth dropped open. "Y-you mean your horses are so wild we have to wear helmets?" She took another step backward, shaking her head.

He grinned at her naïveté. Yep, city girl through and through. He couldn't resist teasing her. "Old Dynamite over there likes to explode and throw off every rider that gets on him. He's the one you'll be ridin'."

"You've got to be kidding." Mariah reached out, grabbing hold of the barn door as if she needed support. She shook her head. "I can't."

He shouldn't be enjoying this so much. "Sure you can. Dynamite only bucks a few times then settles down to a bumpy trot. Course, you gotta watch out for snakes. If he sees one, he goes into a crazy bucking frenzy."

She narrowed her eyes. "Oh, ha-ha. Like he was bucking when that rattler was in here?"

Feeling God's hand of conviction on his shoulder, Jackson set the helmets on a table near the barn door and faced her. "I was just jokin'. Most of those horses are gentle as babies. Still, there are a few that are green—not broken in yet—so you should stay away from those and not handle them."

She nodded slowly, looking relieved. "I don't plan on handling any of them."

Jackson's breath caught at being so close to her. With her looking up at him with those big eyes, he had a fleeting thought that he should wrap his arms around her and kiss away her concerns. Then he stepped away and regained control of his senses. "Are you ready to go?"

"Um…yeah, but I am not riding a horse," she said with renewed determination.

He pulled open the door leading into his attached garage and held out his hand, motioning at his motorcycle. He tossed her a saucy grin. "Maybe you'd feel safer on this."

FOUR

Mariah's gaze zipped toward a sleek, black motorcycle with chrome fenders that gleamed in the garage light. For a moment, she didn't respond, but then her lips tilted up. "Now you're talking."

"Here's your helmet." He handed her the purple one Kelly wore when biking, and she put it on. "Have you ridden before?"

She nodded. "I had a boyfriend in high school who had a bike. Of course, it wasn't as nice as this one. I'm surprised we're riding since it's December. I figured we'd take your truck."

"Can't. Justin took Baron and went to town for supplies." He pushed against the handlebars and booted up the kickstand. "If you'd rather, we can ride four-wheelers, but you'd have to drive one yourself. I don't like going double on them, except with Hailey."

She glanced at the back of the garage, where the three four-wheelers were parked. "No, this is fine. Who's Justin?"

"A college student who works for me part-time." Jackson tugged on his helmet and snapped the chin strap. "So, City Girl, you ready for a tour of my ranch?"

Mariah's eyebrows dipped for a moment at the moniker, but then she shrugged one shoulder. "Sure."

"All right. Hold on to me and lean the way I do when we make a turn."

Mariah blinked, and then her eyes widened. "Hey! I can hear you inside the helmet. Speakers—cool."

"Yep." Jackson hopped on then motioned for her to do the same. He pushed a button, opening the garage door, then gave her a quick tour of the ranch area around the house. Turning onto County Line Road, he revved up the bike, now that Mariah had gotten used to it. Dried grass and oak trees with dead leaves still clinging to their limbs blurred as Jackson sped down the road. He felt free, just like when he raced a horse across the rolling hills of his ranch. Like an eagle soaring high in a brilliant blue sky.

He loved the feel of the wind whipping at his jacket. Even though it was December, the warm weather felt more like early October, and his lightweight jacket kept him plenty warm. That was one thing he loved about winter in Northeastern Oklahoma; there were bound to be some warm days tucked in between the cold ones.

Mariah had sat stiffly when they first got on the motorcycle. She must not have wanted to hold on to him because she had kept her hands on her thighs. Jackson grinned. At least she had until he'd revved the bike forward a few feet, almost knocking her off. She grabbed his waist then and hung on.

He liked that she wasn't using her female wiles to charm him into allowing her to do the story. He wasn't used to women not flirting. Even most of the single women in town and at church had tried to catch his attention at one time or another. Maybe he wasn't Mariah's type—or she wasn't attracted to him because he had a child. He might not be a famous football player anymore, but he liked to think women still found him good-looking. *What does she think about me?*

Pursing his lips, he slowed for a stop sign. Mariah Reyes

was the last woman he should be interested in. She was a reporter who had the power to destroy the peaceful life he enjoyed. If she made public where he lived or wrote what was happening at the ranch, his life could change drastically—and not in a good way. He clenched his jaw. He had no business being attracted to her. *Just stick to the facts, Durant, and send her on her way ASAP.*

"That white house on the right is where Lance lives." He glanced over to admire the changes his friend had made to the old structure that had lain in disrepair for years after its owner died. "That place used to be a dump, but Lance installed new siding and put a roof on it." Jackson's land encircled Lance's on three sides, and though his friend had asked if he'd be willing to sell him fifty acres, he hadn't yet decided.

He'd hoped Lance's moving to Oklahoma would satisfy his need for friendship, but it hadn't completely. Too often lately, he'd been remembering the one good year he'd had with Misty and wishing things had never gone south. He actually missed being married—not that he'd been married all that long. But it had been nice for a while.

Irritated at his train of thought, he twisted the handgrip, and when the bike lurched forward, Mariah's arms tightened around his waist. He blew out a deep breath. Maybe he was lonely.

Sure, he had Hailey and his family and friends. But deep inside, if he was honest with himself, he longed for the love of a woman—one who would love him for himself, not because he'd been famous or because he had some money, but for the man he was. In truth, he had to admit he enjoyed the feel of Mariah's arms locked around his waist and her legs knocking against his when he changed gears. He'd spent a long time avoiding women, and to have one here on the ranch was more troublesome—and pleasant—than he'd imagined.

Spying the broken section of fence, he slowed the motorcycle to a quick stop, causing Mariah to bump against his back and cling tighter. He turned off the engine and stared at the damage. The fence had obviously been cut. Nothing could have broken all three strands of barbed wire in the same place like that without damaging the wooden fence posts.

Had it just been some kids looking for fun?

He removed his helmet. Doubtful. Any teens who lived around here would know how dangerous a cut fence could be, not only to cattle and horses but also to drivers. Besides, most of the local kids were big fans of his and would never damage his property.

Who else, then? He didn't have any enemies—at least not anymore. The only people to even get angry with him lately had been Howard Stunkard and Evan. But neither of them was destructive, although you'd never believe Howard wasn't if you listened to him rant.

None of this made any sense. After Hailey's birth and Misty's death, he'd hightailed it out of Texas to the rolling hills of Northeastern Oklahoma and the ranch he'd inherited from Uncle Dan. He'd earned a place in the community of farmers and ranchers, and even the businessmen in the small town of Westin respected his privacy. He'd made many friends and settled in a church, once he gave his heart to God.

A scissor-tailed flycatcher landed on a nearby fence post, drawing his attention. The gray-and-white bird pecked at something then flew over to a juniper shrub. Jackson peered over his shoulder at Mariah. "Did you see that? It's our state bird."

Mariah removed her helmet. "No, I was studying the landscape. It's hillier here than the Dallas area."

"That's true." Jackson glanced back at the curled barbed wire. Why would someone do this? Even his brother no longer resented that their uncle had left the biggest share of the ranch to him and that Evan had gotten their grandmother's house in town. Uncle Dan had made the right decision. His sister, Kelly, had been able to live in town with Evan and graduate from Westin High, while Jackson had traveled with the Tornados. Evan had set up his computer business in the downstairs of Granny's old house, and thanks to the internet, he owned a booming computer consulting company, even though he lived in a small country town.

Jackson ran his hand through his hair, remembering the sorry state of neglect the ranch had been in when he finally decided to relocate here. Thankfully, by then, Kelly had graduated and moved in to help with baby Hailey. He'd been blessed with a small core group of family and good friends and had no enemies that he could name.

But now, for several weeks, there had been incidences. It made him uneasy. But how did one fight against so many random events?

Mariah's hand tightening on his shoulder jarred him out of his reverie as she eased off the back of the bike. He stood, hauling up the backpack of supplies that he'd secured in front of him, and bit back a grin. Her hair looked as if she'd just crawled out of bed. All messed up and cute.

A faint blush rose to her cheeks when he continued to stare. Breaking the connection, he hung his helmet on the handlebar, rolled his bike onto the road's tarred shoulder and lowered the kickstand, and then he tromped through the tall weeds toward the fence.

He should probably be a gentleman and offer Mariah a hand, but his gaze locked on the clean cut of the wire again. Frustration spiraled through him. He surveyed the area, but the grass was too thick to leave footprints. He didn't fear any of his horses getting loose again, as yesterday, Justin and Lance had helped him round them up and put them in a secure pasture. All but one. After he finished here, he needed to find Princess, the missing mare. She was due to foal any day.

He turned to Mariah as he unzipped the backpack, not surprised to see that she still stood on the edge of the black-topped road, looking uncertain.

"This might take a while," he said. "Why don't you take a walk around and check things out? There's a pretty little creek that runs along the bottom of the valley, just over that hill."

She glanced in the direction he pointed then looked at the ground. "What about snakes?"

"I doubt there's any snakes out here. Too cold for 'em this time of year."

"There was one in your barn."

Jackson scowled at the reminder. "Like you said, I don't believe it got there by accident."

"I could help you—I mean, if you need it."

He looked at her soft hands, not wanting to think what a mess the barbed wire could make of them. "Thanks for the offer, but I only brought one pair of gloves." He pulled them from his backpack and waved them at her.

"All right. I'd like to see that creek. Sounds pretty." A heartwarming smile drove away the apprehension in her expression, and then she hopped across the ditch, stepped past him and went through the opening in the fence. She paused and turned back. "How will I get out if you patch this?"

"I'll hold it open so you can climb through."

She nodded and turned, cautiously picking her way across the uneven ground.

He watched her dark hair swish back and forth as she walked. She must have combed it when he wasn't looking, because it looked close to perfect now. Mariah was slim, but definitely not cheerleader thin. He'd never been attracted to a brunette before. Blondes were more his style.

He screeched on the brakes at that thought, jerked his

gloves on, then reached into his supply bag for his tools. *Get to work, Durant. Don't think about that greenhorn reporter.*

She'd be leaving in a few days anyway. Jackson shook his head. This was why he didn't want women on the ranch. They were a distraction. Nothing but trouble.

Glad that Justin had dropped off a roll of wire and some equipment on his way to town, Jackson started unrolling a section. While he removed the barbs from one end of the wire, he listened to the repetitive tap of a woodpecker on the telephone pole off to his right. The bright sun warmed him, and the comfortable temperature beckoned him to hop back on his bike and ride off toward the horizon. He loved the quiet of the Oklahoma hills, where he felt closer to God than anywhere else he'd been. He loved living close to nature, where things were so peaceful.

A loud crack echoed across the hills. Jackson jumped, nicking his finger on a barb. Gunfire?

He scanned the nearby hills. Two more shots rang out, disrupting the quiet. Deer season ran for another week, but no one had permission to be hunting on his land.

Another blast ripped the quiet, followed by a scream.
Mariah!

Jackson threw down the wire cutters, bolted through the opening in the fence and ran to the nearest oak. The next tree was a good twenty feet away, but he dashed toward it as if he were chasing a goal line. Confusion warred in his mind. He wanted to charge over the hill, but he couldn't help Mariah if he got shot. He hoped she'd taken cover somewhere and stayed put.

He scanned the highest hill to the west, looking for the glint of sunlight off the barrel of a rifle, but saw nothing. One minute passed. Then two. No more shots came.

Had someone been illegally hunting on his land? He didn't want to believe that it could be something more nefarious.

Hunkering down, he raced for the hilltop, running fast, boots thudding on the hard ground. He hurdled several small bushes and lunged to the ground as he reached the crest. He crept forward in the tall grass, hoping it sheltered him from the shooter. He could see the pond but not Mariah. Blood pounded in his ears.

Was she hurt? Lying on the ground, shot?

"Please, God. No."

Five minutes since the last shot. Dare he believe the gunman was gone? Or was the shooter waiting for him to run over the hill?

He couldn't just lie there when Mariah might be hurt. Jackson scanned the area for cover between the hill and pond—but there was precious little. Nothing but a few saplings.

About two hundred yards to his right, a grove of cottonwoods and bald cypress trees followed the creek. He backed down the hill and took off running toward them, hoping the sniper couldn't see him. The dried grass crunched under his feet. He reached the tree line and paused.

Interspersed with the trees, huge limestone boulders jutted up from the ground. At least he had cover here. He dashed to the first giant stone and looked around it. The creek was still a good fifty yards away.

There had been no more gunfire. Had the shooter left? Or was he simply biding his time until he had the right prey in his sights?

"Help us out, Lord."

An instant peace washed through him, and he felt certain the gunman had gone.

"Mariah!" Jackson called out.

"Over here."

His heart lurched at the sound of her voice—and then he saw her peer around a boulder on the far side of the creek. Good girl. She'd taken cover.

"Are you hurt?"

"No. Do you think the shooter is gone?"

"I don't know. Stay there. I'll come to you."

He searched the far hills again and then pushed off the boulder and raced through the trees. The trunks weren't large enough to hide behind, but there were enough of them to deflect a shot, unless the gunman was an expert. He reached the creek, leaped across, then ran to the boulder where Mariah had taken cover and skidded to a halt.

She stood, and his gaze traveled her body, looking for any sign of injury. Her pants were muddy where she'd been kneeling, as were her shoes, but there was no sign of blood. "You're really okay?"

She nodded then sagged toward him, and against his better judgment, he pulled her to his chest. She trembled but didn't cry. He could feel her heart beating fast—she must be terrified. After a few moments of holding him, she swallowed hard and stepped away, her gaze serious. "Someone tried to shoot me."

"How do you know they were shooting at you?"

"Because he nearly got me. I heard something and had gone to investigate. I was standing by the creek when the first shot rang out, and a rock not ten feet from me exploded in pieces." She grabbed his sleeve. "C'mon. I'll show you."

He followed her along the creek bank for a short while then stooped down to examine the flat slab of limestone Mariah pointed at. He wasn't sure he believed her theory that the shooter was aiming for her, but the rock said otherwise. The center of the two-foot-long stone had been hit by something, making a deep groove and shattering part of it. He stood and looked across the hills, trying to determine where the shot had come from. He blew out a sigh. Time to call the sheriff.

Jackson pulled out his phone and dialed his sister's number.

"Hey, big brother. What's up?"

"Can you swing by the school this afternoon and pick up Hailey before she hops on the bus?"

"Sure. Then what?"

"Could you keep her overnight? She'll probably fuss because she wants to spend more time with Mariah, but it's important. Order pizza on me and stay in tonight, okay?"

"You got a hot date?" Kelly giggled.

"Not exactly. Got another favor. Call Sheriff Parker and see if he can come out to the ranch—ASAP."

"What's going on?"

"Can't tell you now. Just do it. Please."

"No fair—"

Jackson hung up. Right now, her knowing nothing was better than knowing the truth. At least he wouldn't have to worry about Hailey.

"I'm beginning to think someone doesn't want me to write your story. What are you not telling me?"

Jackson stiffened and frowned. "Nothing. Seriously. I can't think of anything in my past—not even close—that's worth killing over."

"Maybe they were just trying to scare me off, like that truck driver." She gasped. "What if it was the same person?"

"I don't know." He shoved his hands in his pockets and shrugged. "This is crazy. Nothing like this has happened around here before."

She hiked her chin. "I hope you're not saying it's my fault."

"No. Not at all. Just trying to make sense of it."

Mariah ducked her head. "Sorry. Guess I'm still a bit shook-up. I grew up on the rough side of Dallas, but no one ever took a shot at me."

"Me neither." Jackson smiled, hoping the action would help her relax.

"I imagine all that was shot at you were cameras."

"Yeah, right. You ready to get back?"

Mariah nodded.

A high-pitched squeal snagged Jackson's attention. "That sounds like a young horse."

"That's the noise I was going to investigate when the shooting started."

"Stay here and let me check it out." He started in the direction of the cry, but Mariah shuffled up behind him. He slowed his steps, and she bumped into his arm.

"Sorry. But I'm going with you."

"Okay. Let's check this out then go home."

Jackson strode alongside the creek for several yards, then rounded a curve. Up ahead, he saw Princess. She raised her head and nickered at him.

He stopped, and Mariah halted beside him. "There's Princess, my missing mare. I don't see the foal, but I think the mare has already given birth."

"How can you tell?"

"She's thinner than she was last time I saw her, for one thing." He watched the mare drink from the creek, and then she stepped back and nuzzled something on the ground. Jackson pointed. "Look, there's the foal, on the far side of the mare."

He didn't like how close it was to the water. "Wait here, while I move closer."

She grabbed his sleeve. "Won't the mama horse chase you away?"

"I don't think so. She knows me."

Mariah watched Jackson slowly approach the horse as he cooed softly to her. Though she loved animals, she'd never been around horses. The few she'd gotten close to were part of the Dallas Police Department Mounted Unit that patrolled a couple of special events she had attended, like the State Fair of Texas. Full-grown horses were huge. She didn't fear much, but horses were one thing that rattled her.

She looked through the trees, wondering if the shooter had left or was waiting for them to step out into the open. She crossed her arms, hoping to keep them from shaking. Had the attacker been trying to scare her or shoot her? She swallowed the lump building in her throat. Maybe she should forget this whole thing and go home. She didn't like the idea of giving up and not getting her story, but was she willing to risk her life for it?

The baby horse squealed, and Mariah sidestepped so she could see it. The poor thing lay in the mud and looked to be stuck. The wide-eyed foal kicked its gangly limbs, struggling to rise in the slippery mud at the creek's edge, but then it relaxed and its nose dipped into the water. It jerked its head up and struggled again. If they hadn't arrived when they did, the poor baby might have drowned.

Jackson reached out, and the mare sniffed his palm. He stepped closer and rubbed his hand across her neck. After a few moments, he slipped in front of the mare and stepped around to the far side of the baby. He stooped down, speaking gentle words to the frightened animal. The mama horse nuzzled her baby while Jackson dug in the mud to free it. Soon, he stood and hoisted it into his arms. Flaring its nostrils, the foal jerked and bucked, trying to get away, but after a few seconds, it dropped its head in resigned exhaustion. The mare shook her head and pranced as Jackson walked toward Mariah, carrying the baby, but then she settled and followed him.

"Do you think it will be okay?" She smiled as the baby stared at her with big brown eyes surrounded by long lashes, and its fuzzy ears flicked back and forth. "Kind of cute, isn't it?"

"Most babies are cute. People. Animals. Makes no difference." A wistful smile tilted his lips, and his charming dimples played hide-and-seek.

Mariah wondered if he was remembering Hailey as a newborn. She must have been a doll. Deep down, Mariah was certain Jackson was a good father. In spite of their rocky beginning, she felt her heart softening toward him, but somehow she had to prevent that from happening. She was here to get a story and that was all.

Jackson turned to face her. "You can touch her if you want. Just be gentle."

"Her?"

He nodded.

"I've heard that a colt is a male baby horse, but what do you call a female?"

"A filly."

Holding her breath, she reached out. The filly jerked her head, causing Mariah to jump and yank her hand back.

Jackson chuckled. "Touch her muzzle—the skin around her nose and mouth."

Not wanting to appear a chicken, she reached out, feeling the skin between the filly's nostrils. It was as soft as the velour blanket on her bed at home. Her gaze darted to his. He grinned, causing a strange fluttering in her stomach.

"Soft, huh?"

"Yeah."

Jackson's sapphire gaze softened. "God gave us animals like horses and dogs to enjoy and to make our lives easier. And more fun. Don't let your fear of them keep you from enjoying them."

She stiffened but considered the words he'd all but whispered. She wasn't fearful, only…cautious. If she was afraid, she'd be packing her bags and insisting on a ride to the nearest airport. She'd been shot at, and now she was standing not four feet from a full-grown horse and wasn't trembling. And she had touched the baby.

Shots or no shots, she had the gumption needed to get her story. That was the only reason she was here in the hills of Oklahoma. This article could get her a permanent position as a reporter—even more so now, considering the interesting twist it'd taken. No one knew her in these parts—to shoot at her meant someone was trying to get to Jackson any way they could. She needed to stick around and get her story. When she did, she'd no longer have to go back to hunting for recipes for the food section or writing unchallenging movie reviews.

"We'd better get this little gal to the ranch and check her out. She probably needs to nurse."

"Do you think it's safe to leave the trees?" Mariah stared in the direction from which the shots had come.

"J.D.!" A man hollered and then jogged over the closest hill.

"Justin! I'm glad to see you."

Mariah walked beside Jackson as they wove through the trees and approached his workman. How was it he happened to show up at this precise moment? Could he be the shooter? The timing was almost perfect for someone up in the hills to have driven—or ridden—this far. She studied his relaxed features. If he was the gunman, he sure was a good actor.

Jackson turned to Mariah. "This is Justin Delaney. He works for me part-time."

Mariah nodded at the cowboy, who looked to be in his early twenties.

He tipped his hat then looked back at Jackson. "I stopped to pick up the supplies but saw that the fence hasn't been fixed yet. I thought I'd make sure you were okay." His gaze shifted to Mariah and then past her. "I see you've found Princess."

"Yeah. Her foal was stuck in the mud down by the creek." Jackson stopped suddenly. "Hey, did you hear that gunfire?"

Justin frowned. "What gunfire?"

"About ten minutes ago someone shot at Mariah."

The workman's eyebrows rose, and he looked her way. "Seriously?"

She nodded, unconvinced by his act. Maybe he was the gunman and had come down to check out his victim.

"Yeah," Jackson said. "I'm sure glad you came along when you did. We'll need the truck to get the filly back to the ranch."

"Are you sure it's safe to leave the trees?" Mariah hated sounding like a scaredy-cat, but she'd never been shot at before.

Jackson nodded. "I think so. No one shot at Justin."

"What about the mother horse?" Mariah asked, still not sure she was ready to trust Jackson's workman.

Jackson smiled at her and hoisted the filly up, as if to get a better hold on her. It squealed, and the mare trotted over to investigate. "She'll follow wherever her foal goes."

Mariah stepped away from the mare and refocused on Jackson's warm smile. Her stomach flip-flopped, and she realized she was walking on dangerous ground. She couldn't let herself be attracted to this man even though he'd put himself at risk to come and find her. She had allowed herself to get caught up in the unbridled pleasure of riding Jackson's motorcycle, walking in the pristine field and enjoying the lovely morning. At least until she'd nearly been shot. Now more than ever, she needed to get her story—and then go home.

Focus, Reyes. You will not be swayed by Jackson Durant's good looks and teasing smile. You've got a job to do.

FIVE

Jackson closed the stall gate and smiled at Hailey. Kelly had called at 8:00 a.m., saying Hailey was begging to come home, so he'd caved, but he aimed to keep her close by— and she didn't know it, but she wasn't staying long.

His daughter held a bottle of specially mixed formula with both hands as Lilly—the name she'd given Princess's foal—nursed with a vengeance. Allowing Hailey to help care for the filly had softened the sting of having to separate Princess from her foal, since the vet wanted Lilly on a special formula to help fight off any infection she may have caught from the muddy water she'd swallowed. He thanked God the filly had lived and that Justin had happened along in his pickup, giving them a ride to the ranch while the mare trotted behind the truck. Now Princess was in Lance's barn, where Lilly couldn't hear her whinnies.

He leaned on the stall gate, thinking about their close call yesterday as he watched his daughter. He remembered how frightened he'd been when he thought Mariah had been hurt and how good it felt to hold her in his arms. For a brief moment, he'd caught a glimpse of the real Mariah— the one without the tough exterior. But once they returned home, she had distanced herself from him. He blew out a loud sigh.

Why couldn't he quit thinking about her? She didn't like

dogs or horses. If he was smart, he'd take her to Tulsa, buy a plane ticket and send her back to Dallas before something else happened and she got hurt.

He'd done a fairly good job avoiding women and protecting his heart until his brother had sanctioned Ms. Reyes to do a story about the ranch. And now someone had shot at her. Could the shooting and story be linked in some way? As hard as he tried to make a connection, he couldn't.

His cell phone rang and Jackson tugged it from his pocket. "Angelfire Ranch."

"That you, Durant?"

Jackson cringed at the familiar voice. He didn't have time for this. "Yeah, it's me, Howard."

"Guess you know I'm calling about that rogue horse you sold me."

"Yeah, and I guess you know my feelings about it." Jackson barely avoided giving Howard Stunkard a piece of his mind. Guarantees had their limitations, and Howard believed in pushing those limits way past what was reasonable.

"I'm bringing your horse back, and I want a refund."

"You didn't even buy that horse from me. I sold that gelding to Mike Allenby, and you bought it from him. I can't help it that Allenby has moved out of state." Jackson pushed his hat back on his forehead and swiped the sweat on his brow. "How do you figure I owe you?"

"You trained him, but he ain't worth a plug nickel."

"You're wrong. He was a good cutting horse, but any horse can go rogue if he's mistreated. How many times are we gonna have this conversation?"

"Till you give me my money back." Jackson pulled the phone away from his ear when Howard slammed it down.

He shook his head. What would it take to please that guy? Maybe he should just take the horse back, even though Howard wasn't the person who had originally bought the horse from him. Sure would be better for the four-year-old gelding.

He reached to put the phone in his pocket when it rang again. Evan's number popped up. "Hey."

"Have you talked to the sheriff yet?" Evan shot right to the point as usual.

"No. He was out on a call."

"I still can't believe someone shot at that reporter."

"I was just thinking of sending her home." The idea of Mariah leaving didn't sit with him as well as he'd expected.

"No can do. Angelfire needs the publicity her story will bring."

Jackson gritted his teeth. Was that all Evan cared about? "Think what kind of publicity we'd have gotten if she'd been shot—or worse."

Hailey exited the stall and took Lilly's bottle to the washroom sink. Seeing his daughter helped him maintain control of his temper. He loosened his grip on the cell phone and tried to relax. His comment must have hit home because Evan didn't say anything—which was highly unusual. All his brother wanted was the assurance that his 15 percent of the ranch turned a profit. "I don't know why you think the ranch needs publicity. We're doing fine without it." *I don't need the publicity,* he wanted to say, but Evan wouldn't listen once his mind was set on something.

"Look, how about I come out tonight for dinner and meet this reporter face-to-face? Then we can talk afterward."

"There's no need for talk. I think it's best if she leaves—and soon. I've got enough on my hands with all the weird things that have been happening around here lately without worrying about Mariah."

"Just don't make any hasty decisions. I'll come out tonight. Talk to you later."

"Yeah." Jackson punched the phone's off button. He turned to go check on Hailey, but his gaze landed on Mariah. His gut jolted. She stood just outside the barn door, staring at him, arms crossed, eyes laced with hurt.

He ran his hand through his hair, wishing he'd kept his big mouth shut. Mariah wasn't the real issue; the stress of the strange occurrences around the ranch had him on edge. He hadn't meant for her to overhear his conversation with Evan, but then, he hadn't exactly been quiet. When would he learn to think first and then speak? "Mariah, I—"

"No." She hiked up her chin. "We had a deal. You said I could stay here until my car's repaired—and that's what I intend to do."

"That was before someone took potshots at you."

"I'm still staying." With grace and stubborn pride, she swirled around, tossing her dark hair over her shoulders, reminding Jackson of a spirited mustang—a mustang that needed to be tamed. He watched her march to the house and slam the door.

He lifted his hand to his hip and blew out a sigh. He owed her an apology, and apologizing didn't come easy. He scowled, but then a smile worked its way to his lips. Okay, then, if she was determined to stay, he just might see what he could do about taming that spunky filly—providing she stayed alive long enough.

"Puh-lease, Mariah." Hailey stuck out her bottom lip and begged with her eyes.

An hour had passed since Mariah had overheard Jackson's phone conversation, and she still wasn't ready to see him again, but as she stared at Hailey's pleading expression, her determination to not leave her room wavered. How did Jackson ever say no to her? It was a marvel that the child wasn't spoiled rotten.

"I know you'll love Lilly if you spend some time with her. Come with me out to the barn and see."

Mariah had a hard time imagining that she could ever love a horse. Soft, cuddly kittens were more to her taste.

"Aw, c'mon."

Would they even be safe going outside after what had happened yesterday? She couldn't live with herself if something happened to the girl, but surely it would be all right since Jackson and the sheriff were out there. And she hated feeling vulnerable, like she had as a child. She inhaled a fortifying breath. "Okay." She'd do it, but only to spend time with Hailey, not because the child cajoled her. "Let's go see this baby horse of yours."

"Yippee." Hailey bounced up and down on the bed, jostling Mariah until she thought for sure she was back on Jackson's motorcycle. Finally, the child hopped to the floor and spun around.

"And Lilly's a filly, not a baby horse." She giggled. "Lilly the filly. I just thought of that."

Mariah smiled at the girl and followed her outside and across the yard. Jackson leaned against the sheriff's SUV, though his expression looked anything but relaxed. He glanced at them as they exited the house but then refocused on the lawman. She wondered if he'd told Sheriff Parker about the black truck that had tried to run her off the road, and she considered asking, but Hailey wouldn't welcome the delay.

"Why didn't you call me when these things first started happening?" The sheriff shoved his hands to his waist and eyed Jackson.

Mariah slowed her steps and stopped. She bent down and retied her shoestrings, hoping to hear more of the conversation. She peeked over at Jackson.

Nostrils flaring, he shrugged then crossed his arms. "Didn't realize I was being targeted then."

"Shooting at stock tanks and cutting fences aren't pranks, Jackson. That's destruction of private property. Can you think of anybody who has a vendetta against you? Someone you maybe angered recently?" The stout sheriff stood only about chin-high to Jackson's six-foot-plus frame.

"C'mon, Mariah." Hailey tugged on her sleeve.

She slowly rose. "Sorry, sweetie." She patted the girl's head and moved forward beside her.

"I need to have a look at that fence. Have you already repaired it?" the sheriff asked.

"Yes, but I kept several pieces of wire to show you."

The voices faded as Hailey tugged her toward the back of the barn. As they passed a stall, a horse shoved its big head over the gate and called a greeting. Mariah jumped and moved out of reach. How could anyone love these giant animals? And how did one ever get used to the stifling odors of a barn? She could only imagine how it must reek in the heat of the summer if it smelled this pungent in winter.

"Hi, Justin." Hailey waved at the tall, lean man in the stall to her right. He didn't look at them but gave a grunt of a greeting as he continued brushing a mocha-colored horse.

Jackson's ranch hand had helped get the filly home yesterday, but he'd been anything but friendly to her. His shifty eyes and the way he avoided looking at her sent uneasy chills skittering down Mariah's arms. Could someone working on the ranch be responsible for Jackson's problems? It would be convenient for the perpetrator, but what could be his motive? That would be like biting the hand that fed you.

Her reporter's instinct told her there was more to this Justin fellow than met the eye. She'd have to do some research on Jackson's ranch hand—if she didn't decide to pack up and leave. She'd lain awake several hours last night reliving the shooting. Was she stupid to stay? If she asked Jackson to take her to Tulsa, she could get a flight and be home in less than an hour. But since becoming an adult and getting her own place, she'd never backed down from a fight. Then again, no one had shot at her before.

Hailey opened a stall and stepped in. "Close the gate so Lilly doesn't get out."

Mariah snagged the swinging door and latched it shut. Over the stall slats, she watched Justin brush the horse with long, broad strokes. Slowly, his head turned in her direction at the same moment something warm and moist licked the back of her hand. She squealed and looked down at the baby horse then fell against the gate. Lilly's head jerked up, startled by her sudden movement. She snorted and backed away. Hailey giggled, and Mariah was almost certain she heard Justin chuckle.

"She won't hurt you. She just likes the saltiness of your skin." Hailey scratched Lilly between her long ears.

Mariah stared at her hand. The dampness glistened in the sunlight flowing through the window behind the stall. She'd never been a diva, but…eww! Horse slobber. Not wanting to wipe it on her clean jeans, she glanced around for a rag.

Lilly wobbled toward her again, head bobbing. Mariah pressed against the gate, wishing she hadn't locked herself in. The filly nuzzled her shirt with her lips. Mariah's heart stopped when she glimpsed Lilly's teeth. She swallowed hard, hoping to escape before the creature snagged a bite of her stomach.

"Don't be afraid. She won't hurt you," Hailey cooed to her like Jackson had spoken to Lilly yesterday when she'd been so frightened.

Mariah wanted to ask how anything with teeth so big could be harmless, but her embarrassment that this young girl was braver than she was held her silent. Lilly seemed gentle enough. In fact, the little horse merely acted curious. Sucking in a breath of courage, she reached out her hand. Lilly sniffed it then snorted. Mariah yanked her hand back, her heart throbbing faster than the peppy salsa music her best friend enjoyed.

To her right, she glanced over to see Justin leading the mocha horse out of the stall. He walked with his head down, shaking it back and forth as he exited the barn. Obviously, he thought she was just as citified as Jackson did. Everything here was new to her, and she hated being judged because of her reaction to things so different from what she was used to. Change had never come easy for her.

Mariah looked down into the trusting brown eyes of the curious young horse. The creature didn't have a mean bone in its body. It was stupid for her to be scared.

She reached out and touched Lilly's velvety nose like she had the day before. The horse nudged her hand, tickling Mariah's palm with exploring lips.

"I think she likes you." The girl's eyes twinkled.

Mariah smiled. She scratched between the filly's ears like Hailey had done. The horse took a step forward and rubbed her head against Mariah's tummy, loosening a chuckle from deep within. Why had she been afraid of this cute little creature?

"Let's take Lilly for a walk," Hailey said. The girl slipped from the stall, leaving Mariah alone with Lilly for a few heart-skipping moments. When she returned, she carried something resembling a green nylon dog leash. She snapped one end onto the red thing strapped on Lilly's head.

Thinking of yesterday's shooting, she shook her head. "I'm not sure it's a good idea to leave the barn."

"I guess we can lead her in the alley between the stalls."

"But isn't she too young?"

Hailey shrugged. "She has to start sometime."

Satisfied, Mariah forced her attention back on the young girl as she instructed her how to lead Lilly.

She smiled at how grown-up the six-year-old sounded. Was it because she was around adults most of the time?

Mariah rolled the lead like Hailey had shown her and tugged on it. Lilly walked through the stall gate then stopped.

The little horse whinnied as Hailey strode out the barn, and suddenly, the filly lunged for the open door. The lead rope uncoiled and slipped through Mariah's fingers. At the last second, she snagged hold of the loop on the end and raced after the filly, who followed Hailey outside.

She squinted from the glare of the afternoon sun as she jogged out of the barn. After a moment, she saw Hailey walking toward her father. The sheriff's vehicle was gone, and Jackson stood next to Justin, examining the mocha-colored horse.

Hailey stopped in front of her father with her hands fisted on her hips. She shook her head, and Mariah was certain she heard the word *greenhorn*. The girl turned and stared at her, looking like a stern schoolteacher. "Looks like Lilly's taking Mariah for a walk."

Jackson and Justin exchanged amused looks, making Mariah feel even more inept. Justin laughed, but Jackson captured her gaze as Lilly slowed to a stop in front of Hailey. He flashed her the smile that she was certain had stolen the hearts of female football fans all across the nation. Only this time, the smile was for her, and it held something else—a hint of pride maybe.

In that instant, she felt sure she would hop on the wildest horse at Angelfire Ranch—if only Jackson would grin at her like that again.

Watching Mariah being pulled along by Lilly sent rippling waves of delight washing through Jackson and released some of his pent-up tension. Maybe she was less fearful than he'd thought. He'd figured she was still in her bedroom, fuming about the phone conversation she'd overheard, until he'd looked up and saw her following Hailey to the barn. He shouldn't have given in to his temper when he was talking to Evan. Getting angry always caused problems. Glancing skyward, he tossed up a request that God would help him maintain control. He was either hot or cold—with him there was no middle ground. If he focused on a task, he put his all into it, and that fortitude was exactly what had enabled him to excel in football.

Lilly stopped in front of Hailey and nudged her shoulder. His daughter giggled as she watched Mariah jog to catch up to them. Mariah's charming grin sent his heart into overdrive. She really was a beauty when she was relaxed and not arguing with him, but he had to admit he liked her dark eyes alive with passion and conviction.

He watched her coil up the lead rope in sloppy circles and hand it to Hailey.

"You did good," his daughter said, with a twinkle in her eye. "Keep at it and maybe you'll be walking Lilly instead of her walking you."

"Ha-ha." Mariah's fake laugh was laced with sarcasm. "Give me some time. This is my first chance to lead something almost as big as I am." Mariah patted the foal's head then fluffed up Lilly's spiky mane. She peered over the filly's neck and flashed Jackson a proud smile.

He chuckled. Maybe there was hope for this city gal.

"Now you try again," Hailey said.

Jackson glanced across the hills, uneasy at having Hailey and Mariah so exposed. He had no choice about being outside. He had a ranch to run, but he wouldn't risk their lives. "Take the horse back to the barn. Then you two need to return to the house."

Mariah's grin wilted. "Your father is right."

"But why?" Hailey asked. "I want to play with Lilly."

Jackson shook his head. "Lilly needs to rest after being stuck in the mud. Take her back."

"Yes, sir." Hailey did as ordered with Lilly and Mariah following.

If he didn't know better, he would never guess someone had tried to use Mariah for target practice yesterday. But someone had. Jackson searched the surrounding hills. Was his adversary out there watching them?

He had hoped to get Mariah on a horse before she left, but riding was out of the question now.

The ta-dump of tires crossing the cattle guard grabbed his attention, and he turned to see a trio of vehicles moving up his gravel road. Jackson frowned. More people at the ranch meant more targets should his nemesis decide to attack again.

Evan's basic blue two-door coupe in the lead kept Lance's shiny Camaro from going as fast as it normally would. Evan would spend big bucks to buy top-of-the-line computer equipment but drive his old car to death. Lance, on the other hand, had to buy a brand-new vehicle every year or two. Behind them, Kelly brought up the rear in her older-model cherry-red Jeep. Jackson was almost surprised there weren't more cars coming, now that word of yesterday's shooting had probably gotten around town.

Baron loped across the pasture and barked a greeting, then trotted over and leaned against Jackson's leg. He licked Jackson's hand then ran back to follow the Camaro with his tail wagging.

The vehicles pulled in side by side. Lance hopped out first and whistled. Baron trotted over with a dog smile on his furry face. As usual whenever he visited, Lance slipped the animal a doggie treat. He scratched Baron behind his ears, then turned and walked toward Jackson. Baron nudged Lance's hand again, then trotted over, tail wagging and tongue flapping, to where Kelly was exiting her Jeep.

Lance scanned the yard, and a smile tugged at his mouth when he spotted Mariah coming out of the barn. Evan also turned in the same direction and stared at her. An uncomfortable feeling unlike any Jackson had experienced in years churned within him. Jealousy?

Nah. Surely not.

Kelly walked beside Evan, also gawking at Mariah. Jackson knew just what they were thinking. Evan was wondering how good a reporter Mariah was and what kind of story she'd write about the ranch. Kelly was probably already matchmaking and scheming how to get him and Mariah together. Jackson shook his head. This was going to be an interesting evening.

Talking with Hailey, his greenhorn hadn't even noticed she was drawing a crowd like flies at a barbecue. Lance made a beeline toward Mariah.

"Hola, señorita." He smiled and stopped in front of her. Jackson's gut churned. Mariah glanced up, her dark brows scrunched in confusion as she noticed the crowd for the first time. Her gaze darted to Jackson, then back to Lance.

His friend tipped his hat. "You glad to see me again, *señorita?*"

Mariah's smile didn't quite reach her eyes. She obviously didn't like him invading her space—and neither did Jackson. Lance didn't take the hint but leaned down in her face, whispering something to her. Her cheeks reddened, and she cast a pleading glance in Jackson's direction.

Gritting his teeth, he moved toward them. There might not be anything between him and the reporter, but he sure wasn't willing to let Lance pester her.

SIX

Jackson marched toward Lance.

"Whoa now. Just hold on there, J.D., ole buddy," Lance said, turning away from Mariah and raising his palms in the air.

With Lance's back turned, Mariah moved toward Jackson, an expression of relief on her pretty face.

Jackson slowed his pace now that she seemed okay.

"I was just giving our guest a friendly Oklahoma greeting. Besides, I think she probably needs to come stay with me. She'd be a lot safer."

Jackson stopped. Mariah might be safer from the gunman at Lance's house, but who'd protect her from her host?

Lance was his best friend, but sometimes he pushed the limits too far. Yes, Lance was cocky and enjoyed the attention of pretty women, but Jackson wouldn't allow his friend to make a guest uncomfortable.

Mariah stopped next to Jackson, while Hailey jogged over to give Kelly a hug. He felt the warmth of her nearness and took a calming breath as his heart kicked into a gallop.

Evan and Kelly stopped between Jackson and Lance, forming a loose circle. Either on purpose or unwittingly, Mariah inched closer to him, the back of her hand brushing against his. With fortitude, Jackson resisted the impulse to grasp hold of it.

Yeah, Mariah was pretty, and he had to admit she intrigued him, too, especially when those dark eyes sparked with excitement or anger. But she was leaving in a few days. Nothing would happen between him and the reporter. His one and only attempt at marriage had ended in a disaster, and he wasn't willing to risk that happening again.

Jackson clenched his teeth, resisting the urge to yank off his hat and slam it against his thigh at the memory of his wife's desertion. Why was it that women stirred up such feelings in men?

The Bible said God made woman to be a helpmate to man, but as far as he could tell, they mostly created problems—like intruding on his privacy. He was safer avoiding females altogether—and that was just what he'd been doing until Evan sent a female reporter here. He scowled in his brother's direction. How could he enjoy Mariah's company and at the same time resent her intrusion? The thought boggled his mind.

"So, you gonna introduce us?" Kelly stared at him, her blue eyes dancing with nothing but trouble.

"She's the reporter," Evan said in his matter-of-fact way.

He could always count on his brother to state the obvious.

Mariah nodded and held out her hand. "I'm Mariah Reyes, reporter for the *Dallas Observer*."

"Evan Durant," he said, shaking her hand.

"I'm Kelly, their sister. I keep these two old coots in line."

Mariah's smile lit her countenance as she shook hands with Kelly. Jackson cocked his head, wondering how the two women would get along. His sister was probably happy to have another female her age to balance out the odds. Most everyone liked Kelly, though as a little sister, she could be typically annoying. And like Lance, she could come on a bit too strong at times.

"So, what do you think of our fine ranch?" Evan asked, as he swept his arm in a half circle. "Jackson's made lots of improvements since he's taken over."

Watching his brother's face beaming with pride, Jackson took a brief moment to relish Evan's rare compliment. His brother had his own ideas for the ranch, even though Evan and Kelly owned only 15 percent each while Jackson owned 70. That was the way of an older brother—always bossing the younger siblings. "Let's head for the house. No sense standing around out here." Where they all had targets on their backs.

Evan nodded and starting walking, sticking close to Mariah. "J.D. has done a good job of getting a base herd of horses and now has weekend sales 'bout every month or so." His brother nodded toward the far pasture, where more than a dozen horses grazed.

Jackson shuffled along, trying to decide whether to stop Evan or let him continue. A part of him still wasn't ready to let Mariah do the story, so he hadn't been too free with info about the ranch, but his brother's rare affirmation was a balm to his soul. Leaving his high-profile football career to settle on a secluded ranch and raise a baby daughter alone had been hard going at first. Well, he hadn't actually been alone, but having the assistance of an often highly emotional teenage sister had been more trouble than help many times.

The screen door banged as they approached the house, and all eyes turned toward the porch, where Deuce stood with his fists on his hips. "Is all them folks eatin' dinner here tonight? I told you to tell me early on when you're havin' company."

Jackson scanned the group, seeing the hopeful, unspoken requests in each person's expression. He nodded at Deuce, who shook his shaggy head and went back into the house, mumbling, screen door slamming behind him.

Jackson had known Evan was coming out to meet Mariah and would probably stay for dinner, but between the sheriff's visit and watching Mariah with the filly, he'd forgotten to mention it to Deuce. Lance's and Kelly's arrivals had been a surprise.

"He's a good cook, but kind of a funny man," Mariah said, as if unsure of whether or not to voice her opinion.

All heads turned back to her, and her eyebrows lifted, daring someone to disagree with her.

"You're right." Kelly nodded, grinning as she grabbed Evan's arm and leaned against him. "His fried chicken is to die for. And wait until you taste his steaks. We raise beef here besides horses, you know."

"Is that his real name?" Mariah asked.

The group chuckled, but Jackson narrowed his eyes, wondering if her question was mere curiosity or if she was searching for information.

"No." Kelly grinned, shaking her head. "His real name's Sherman."

"And he has a twin brother named Herman," Lance said.

Amusement twinkled in Mariah's dark eyes. "Sherman and Herman. That's almost cruel."

Kelly laughed. "Guess that's why he goes by Deuce and his older brother is known as Ace."

"I'm not sure if that's all that much better." Mariah grinned.

The group of family and friends shared a little laugh at Deuce's expense, though Jackson held back. It wasn't as if he had a lot of room to talk about odd names since he bore his mother's maiden name for his moniker.

The sun ducked behind a cloud, and a chilly gust blew across the ranch yard.

"Brrr! It's getting colder out. Feels more like December now," Kelly said, shoving her hands in the pockets of her leather jacket. She jogged up the porch steps.

"Hey, wait for us, Aunt Kelly," Hailey called, as she grabbed Mariah's hand and tugged her toward the porch. A wave of fatherly pride swelled in Jackson's chest. He loved his daughter so much at times he could hardly hold in his swirling emotions.

"Wow. She's hot." Evan slowed his pace, shoved his hands in his pockets and started jingling the coins hidden deep in the shadows.

"You got that right," Lance said.

Jackson scowled at his friend and then his brother.

Evan turned a surprised look his way. "Don't tell me you haven't noticed how attractive she is."

He'd noticed. But he wasn't going to admit it—not here— not now. And he certainly didn't want his brother or Lance noticing.

"So, someone really took a shot at her?" Evan lifted one eyebrow.

"Yes, I'm certain. And not just one—closer to a half dozen. I heard them."

Evan let out an impressed whistle.

"How do you know it wasn't a hunter?" Lance asked.

"If it was, he was hunting Mariah—or at the least trying to scare her away. Barely missed her twice, from what I could tell."

"That's certainly not good for business." Evan frowned. "Why would someone want to shoot at her? No one even knows she's here."

"People know." Lance leaned against a fence post, arms folded. "Don't forget we live in a small county, and word gets around."

Both brothers turned their stern gaze on Lance.

"Hey, don't blame me." He held up his palms in defense. "You called Denton's office. The sheriff and his deputies know. She stopped at the Tank Up on the way to the ranch. Lots of folks saw her."

Jackson pushed his hat up off his forehead. More people than he'd realized were aware of his guest. "Okay, but who would have reason to not want her here?"

Lance remained silent for once, and Evan shrugged.

"Well, as soon as her car is fixed, she's out of here. I have enough to worry about besides a greenhorn from the city."

Evan jingled his coins faster. "You still want me to take her off your hands?"

Jackson blinked. It took a moment before he remembered their phone conversation. Did he want to be rid of Mariah?

Yes.

Maybe.

No.

At least if she was here, he could control the flow of information she received. There was no telling what Evan might tell her. And he could protect her far better than his brother, who didn't even own a gun.

"Hey." Lance nudged Jackson's arm with his elbow. "I asked first."

"No," he said, matching his brother's actions and shoving fingertips in his tight pockets. "She can stay here. Hailey likes her." *I like her.*

Jackson hoped his heart would still be intact when Mariah left. Something about the reporter drew him like a June bug to a porch light. Maybe it was the loneliness he recognized in her whenever she dropped her reporter facade, because he felt the same way. How could he be surrounded by a loving family and still feel isolated?

"If you change your mind, just remember I offered first." Lance's grin slackened. "So, has she written her story yet?"

Jackson knew Lance had just voiced Evan's unasked question. "No, and I'm not so sure she's going to."

"Why not?" His brother scowled. "I went to a lot of trouble to get a reporter here."

"Maybe you should have mentioned the reporter was a woman." Jackson faced his brother head-on.

"You would never have agreed."

Jackson frowned. "So you *did* know in advance. You kept it a secret and let her come here, knowing how I feel about women. Knowing how important my privacy is."

Evan held up his hands in surrender. "Now hold your horses, J.D. That's not true. I honestly thought the *Observer* was sending a man. I never even considered they might send a female reporter to do a story on a former pro athlete."

He released a long sigh, allowing the tension to flow out of him as he saw the truth in his brother's eyes. Evan hadn't known Mariah was a female. Lance stood with his arms crossed over his chest, having no qualms about eavesdropping. Well, it wasn't the first time his friend had seen him and Evan arguing.

"So, you two agree that neither of you knew a female reporter was coming?" Lance asked, suddenly the arbitrator.

Jackson eyed his brother a final time, then nodded the same instant Evan did.

"Good. Now that that's settled," Lance said, "do you think Mariah would want to go out with me tomorrow night?"

Mariah stared in disbelief at the newspaper article she'd pulled up on her laptop. Jackson wanted her to leave but he allowed Justin to work on his ranch when the young man had such a criminal past. According to this article, written after his last brush with the law, Justin had started out with simple graffiti painting that had escalated into destruction of school property and then armed robbery of a convenience store. Another search for his name told her that after a short term in a youth detention center, Justin had been sent to one of those boot camps for juvenile offenders. He was fortunate that he'd been a minor when he'd committed his crimes or he probably would still be in prison.

Leaning back in her chair, she yawned and glanced at the clock. 11:40. She needed to hit the hay soon, but she wasn't done yet. She drummed her fingers on the desk. Could Justin be causing Jackson's problems? Obviously, he had the history and ability to be destructive, but what could be his motive? Could Jackson have had anything to do with Justin getting arrested and being sent to jail? But if that was true, why in the world would Justin be working at Angelfire now?

She scanned several other articles, hoping for new information. The only other pertinent fact was that Justin had been in the same high school graduation class as Kelly. Interesting.

She clicked the word-processing tab at the bottom of her computer to open her file and stared at her list of suspects. She highlighted Justin's name and moved him to the top.

She'd already researched Lance Jordan. Westin's weekly newspaper held a wealth of information on him and Jackson. Evidently, Lance's biggest problem was his loose mouth— that and drinking too much on the weekends. He'd gotten arrested for DUI once last June while at summer football camp in Dallas. That had resulted in him losing a lucrative advertising contract. Then he'd gotten injured in the second game this year and was out for the season and had been sent home to recover. Last month his mother died, and he'd had to settle her estate. Now he was back in Oklahoma. He'd had a run of bad luck, but as far as she could tell, none of it was tied to Jackson.

She picked up the articles that she'd printed on her portable printer and studied them. Lance had joined the Tornados the same year as Jackson. Though Jackson was selected as starting quarterback his second year with the Tornados, it took Lance another year to become a starting receiver. Their careers paralleled each other's, and they'd become good friends, but it seemed odd to Mariah that Lance would buy a ranch next door to Jackson's. She'd never had a super-close friend and couldn't imagine wanting to live next door to one.

Mariah rolled her head around, stretching her neck muscles. Stifling a yawn, she clicked on the article she'd started on Jackson. She'd noticed she was the only one who called him by his first name. Everyone else referred to him as J.D. Course, that was the name the world knew him as—J. D. Durant—star quarterback of the Texas Tornados.

She could understand how losing his wife and being left the single father of a newborn daughter was enough to cause him to walk away from a football team on the way to the Super Bowl. Some Tornado fans still grumbled about him not following through on his contract and quitting near the end of an undefeated season. They blamed him for the Tornados losing in the play-offs. They had cared more for their team winning the Super Bowl than they had for their hurting quarterback.

A vehicle rumbled to life outside her window. She recognized the loud, vibrating sound of Lance's Camaro. He was leaving. Mariah heaved a sigh of relief. She couldn't deny Lance's charming good looks, but his personality was sorely lacking. She hated come-on jocks who were full of themselves. They reminded her of her brother. And thoughts of Carlos were never pleasant. He was too much like their abusive father.

Mariah shook her head, hoping to rid it of thoughts of her dysfunctional family. She needed to concentrate on Jackson's, not hers. Kelly was a cutie. She had felt an instant connection with Jackson's sister. They'd chatted over dinner about the latest fashions and included Hailey in their conversation as much as possible. Given the chance, she and Kelly could probably become friends. Mariah hated to see Kelly take Hailey home with her tonight, but it was the smart thing. She would miss Jackson's precocious daughter, but her safety was the priority—and she was safer away from the ranch for now.

She stared at Evan's name on her laptop. He was an older and thinner version of Jackson, more studious-looking and less brawny. Both men—in fact, all three siblings—sported the same almost-black hair and dark blue eyes. Jackson's brother was still on her list of suspects. While it was unlikely he had anything to do with the problems on the ranch, he still had motive. Jackson mentioned Evan being upset about their uncle leaving only a small percentage of the ranch to him and Kelly, while the lion's share had gone to Jackson. Though Evan didn't seem the kind of person to hide guilt well, Mariah wasn't ready to rule anyone out yet.

Tomorrow, when she wasn't so tired, she'd see if she could track down something on Deuce. She also had to consider that maybe the target wasn't Jackson—maybe someone at the *Observer* was out to get *her*. Her gut told her no, that the shooting and black-truck incidents were related to Jackson's troubles, but she had to consider all the possibilities.

Swiping her tongue around her dry mouth, she suddenly realized how thirsty she was. She pushed back her chair, stood and stretched. A cold glass of ice water was just what she needed.

Mariah peeked out her bedroom door. The house rested beneath a blanket of darkness. Jackson and Deuce were most likely in bed by now. She turned toward the living area, where a faint light glowed from Jackson's office. Probably a night-light.

Tiptoeing down the hall so as not to wake anyone, she heard a faint mumbling as she drew near the office door. Her heart somersaulted at the closeness of a voice. She peered through the open doorway, her eyes taking a moment to adjust to the muted darkness. A dark figure huddled on its knees, leaning over the couch seat, forehead resting in hands. Jackson.

"And, Lord, I really need Your help…"

Immediate guilt lanced Mariah when she realized she'd caught him praying. She shouldn't listen to a man's conversation with God, but something held her immobile.

"Help me discover the source of the problems here. Guide me to the person responsible, and thank You for protecting my family—and Mariah. I pray for Your continued protection. Property can be replaced, but not people."

Mesmerized, Mariah continued to listen. She looked around the dimly lit room, almost expecting to see someone else sitting in the shadows. How could Jackson talk to God just like he would a friend? The few church services she'd sat through before her mother died had been long and boring liturgical recitations, and nobody had dared pray to God in such an informal manner. Could this be what people meant when they said God was their friend?

Guilt for eavesdropping finally overpowered her curiosity. She tiptoed past the doorway.

"Forgive me again, Lord, for being angry with Evan and losing my temper over this situation with Mariah."

She stopped in midstride at Jackson's soft entreaty.

"I know there must be a reason You sent her here. I just need to be patient. Show me whether or not I should allow her to do the story." Jackson heaved a sigh. The gentle glow from his desk lamp illuminated his shoulders. His fingers plowed through his hair and came to rest on the back of his head. "Maybe it's time I quit hiding out from the real world."

His soft chuckle startled Mariah after the serious tone of his prayer. The excitement that coursed through her, knowing that he was at least considering cooperating with her on the story, warred with her yearning not to be the one to rock his peaceful world, as the article was certain to do.

Once loyal fans and the media discovered where he'd been hiding all these years, there would surely be at least some who would seek him out and pester him.

He chuckled again. "Yes, I know You've been after me for a while to quit hiding out here on the ranch. I'm listening. It's just taken time for the idea to soak into my thick brain. And, Father…" Jackson paused, as if debating his next prayer. "Help me to keep this attraction to Mariah in proper perspective."

Mariah's heart jumped again. His attraction to her? She blinked. *He's attracted to me?* Swallowing hard, she struggled to keep the pulsating beat of her heart from echoing so loudly that Jackson would hear it. Now she desperately wanted to know his next words.

But why did she care so much? Was she actually attracted to this man? Sure, he was handsome and had a nice home and a sweet child, but he could be cranky and insensitive—but then, who wasn't at least some of the time?

"Thanks for Your blessings, Lord. In Jesus's name, Amen."

Oh, no! She'd gotten so caught up realizing she actually liked Jackson Durant that she'd missed the rest of what he'd said. He breathed another sigh, as if satisfied with his prayer time, and then he stretched and yawned. With a glance at his watch, he unfolded his long body off the floor and rose to his feet.

Apprehension at getting caught watching and listening to him spurred Mariah's feet into action. She sped softly toward the kitchen and banged straight into the table.

SEVEN

Jackson's heart took a frenzied leap the same time his body catapulted into action. Someone was in his kitchen! He flew out the office door, skidding around the corner on his sock-clad feet, and flipped on the light. He blinked as his eyes adjusted from the muted dimness of his office to the stark brightness of the kitchen.

"Oh, ow. Ow!" Mariah held on to the table with one hand, hopping around on her left foot. She leaned forward and grasped the toes of the other foot that hung useless in midair. Pain contorted her pretty features. "Oh, man, that hurt."

"Sit down," he ordered. Why in the world had she been wandering around the house with the lights off?

Jackson grabbed a small sandwich bag from a box in the cabinet and filled it with crushed ice from the refrigerator door. Yanking out the chair next to Mariah's, he plopped down then pulled her foot onto his knee. He laid the ice bag over her toes and looked up into her surprised face.

She tried to tug her foot away, but he held on tight. "I—I can do that myself."

"I know, but I'm getting used to patching you up." He smiled, and her brow scrunched in confusion. Good. Keep her too rattled to ask questions. "So, what are you doing up this late?"

"What are *you* doing up so late?" She tipped her chin in the air and glared at him.

Touché! "Praying."

Mariah blanched. "That's—uh—nice." She broke eye contact and glanced away.

He wondered about her odd reaction, but she wasn't the first person he knew who felt funny talking about prayer. "Did you need something from the kitchen?"

She licked her lips, and Jackson felt as if a bucking bronco had been turned loose in his belly. "I just wanted some cold water before going to bed."

"Why didn't you turn the light on?"

Mariah shrugged. "With Deuce's room on the other side of the kitchen, I wasn't sure if the light shining under his door would awaken him."

"Nothing short of a tornado could wake Deuce once he's taken off his hearing aid." Lifting her foot, he eased out of the chair then set her heel on the seat. The ice bag rested across her toes. He retrieved a bottle of water from the fridge and handed it to her.

"Thanks." Taking the bottle, Mariah flashed a little smile, twisted off the cap and took a long swig.

Lifting her foot onto her opposite knee, she laid the ice bag on the table, then pulled off her satiny slipper and white slouch sock and massaged her little toe. Jackson stared, mesmerized by her tiny feet. Misty's feet had been long and wide, with toes so limber she could pick up dimes off the tile floor with them. Jackson shook his head. He didn't want to compare the two women. One was gone forever and the other would soon leave. He didn't want to think about that, either.

"Shouldn't you keep the ice on it?"

Mariah shook her head. "No, it's feeling better already. Thanks for fixing the pack, though."

He nodded, then took the ice bag and tossed it in the sink. "You and Kelly seemed to get along well tonight."

"Your sister's really sweet. I like her." Mariah's eyes gleamed like onyx stones polished to a glistening shine. "I was surprised by how you all look so much alike."

Jackson thought a moment. Did they resemble each other? He'd never actually paid that much attention to his siblings' features.

"You all have the same dark hair and similar blue eyes. And even though you're younger than Evan, you're taller and…" A faint stain colored Mariah's cheeks.

And what…? Jackson leaned forward, willing her to finish her sentence.

Mariah pulled her sock on, followed by her dainty slipper. Picking up the water bottle, she stood, gently testing her injured foot. "Almost good as new."

Obviously she wasn't going to finish whatever it was she'd started to say. This was the first time all evening he'd had her to himself, and he wasn't ready to let her go yet.

"Can you walk on it—or do you need me to carry you?" He didn't even try to hold back the ornery grin that tugged at his lips.

Blushing, she shrugged. "N-no. See, it's fine." As if trying to prove it to herself, she hobbled away a few steps. "Just a little bruised."

Jackson stood and crossed to her side. "If it's really feeling all right, there's something I'd like to show you."

Mariah nodded, curiosity dancing in her eyes.

"We'll have to step outside onto the porch. It's cold out there. Is that okay?"

"Sure, but do you think it's safe—after what happened?"

"I'll turn out the lights so no one can see us."

She glanced at the front door, contemplated a moment and then nodded. "Okay, but I need to get my shoes."

Jackson handed her a pair of battered boots. "Try these. You can probably leave your slippers on."

She slid her feet into the boots and looked up. "They're a bit big, but not too bad. Whose are they?"

"Deuce's." Jackson grinned.

Her eyebrows shot up. "And you don't think he'd mind me borrowing them?"

"No, I don't." Holding on to her elbow, he guided her to the coatrack as she hobbled along. After they donned their jackets, he slipped on his boots and flipped off the kitchen and mudroom lights. Then he helped her outside past the creaking screen door.

"Brrr. It gets cold here when the sun goes down." She zipped her jacket and pulled the collar up around her neck.

"Pretty typical weather for early December, although we haven't had a hard freeze yet."

Guiding her over to the porch railing, he kept his hand on her elbow, just in case she should stumble.

"What's making that noise? Not a cricket."

"Tree frogs. There are only a few still around this late, but you should hear them in the summer." Jackson tilted his chin upward. "What I wanted to show you is up there."

Mariah lifted her eyes to gaze at the night sky. "Oh, wow! Look at all the stars," Mariah said on a whispered breath. "I didn't know there were so many."

"Pretty amazing. Huh?"

"Yeah. There's millions of them." Tilting her face skyward, Mariah leaned against the porch railing, her breath steaming out in a puff.

Jackson stood behind her and looked up. The moon was nowhere to be seen, but the myriad stars gave off their own gentle illumination. Mariah was so close he could envelop her in a hug if he simply locked his arms around her. He shook his head, fighting his attraction. It had been a long time since a woman had intrigued him, but this one was off-limits.

"Uh…" He cleared his throat, trying to regain control of

his emotions. Coming outside had been a bad idea. "Can I ask you something?"

"Sure, I guess."

"I don't know anything about you. Have you always lived in Dallas?"

"Yep, born and raised there."

"Got any family? Siblings?"

Her breathing deepened, and she was quiet for a long moment. "Just a father and brother. My mom died when I was twelve."

He sensed there was more she wasn't saying but didn't press her. "Sorry about your mom. My folks both died in a car wreck when I was twenty-three. I was playing pro ball then." And had barely had time to grieve. Misty had comforted him when no one else had, and that had led to their brief courtship and marriage.

"I really miss my mother. I imagine you feel the same about your parents."

"Yes, I do, especially when I think how much they would have loved Hailey."

She turned his way. "My turn to ask questions."

Anxiety tightened his shoulders. "Fair enough. Shoot."

She huffed out a laugh. "Nice choice of words, considering. When did your ranch problems first start?"

He thought back. "It's hard to say. I guess the first thing was about three weeks ago, when I got a call that some of my horses were on County Line Road. That was the first time the fence had been cut."

"Did you contact the sheriff?"

"No. I thought it was just someone being ornery. It happens occasionally."

"Had it happened before?"

"Um…no. But I've known others who had the same problem—but no one lately."

Mariah leaned against the porch railing. "And you still can't think of anyone who might have a vendetta?"

He'd thought long and hard and still came up with the same answer. "Nope."

"You're smart to send Hailey back to your sister's." She sucked in a breath then exhaled loudly. "I don't want to alarm you, but I'm sure you've noticed the attacks are escalating. Someone wants to cause you—or maybe even me—harm. I just can't figure out if the shooting is related to the other events."

"Why would anyone want to harm you?" That made no sense to him.

"No clue, unless it's someone at work who's worried that my story will get me promoted to the position they want. But attacking me seems overly harsh, considering the two people in line for the job."

No wonder she wanted this story so badly. It meant a possible promotion. How could he begrudge her that? She was on her own and had to do what she could to move up the ladder, just as he had when playing football.

"I want you to know that I'll do all I can to help figure out this dilemma."

Without stopping to think, he took her hand. "I appreciate that." Warmth curled around him as he grasped her soft hand. He hadn't relied on many people in his adult years, since so many proved false. In the football world, it had been dog-eat-dog. Do your best or someone would eagerly take your place. He'd learned to rely on himself—at least until he gave his heart to God. He longed to trust Mariah, but her story stood between them.

"Brrr. The temperature sure did drop."

He wrapped his arm around her shoulders, hoping the warmth of his body would take the chill away. He was surprised when she eased against him.

"Um… Is that the Big Dipper?"

He glanced up and nodded. "Yeah."

"Cool. I don't know that I've seen it before in real life. Books, of course." She turned toward him, and her breath touched his cheek like a feather. "With all the lights in Dallas, we can only see a few stars."

Mariah's closeness froze his brain.

"Thank you for bringing me out—" She stopped talking, as if she suddenly realized she'd been leaning on him and now they stood face-to-face.

Was she bothered by his nearness? When she'd first arrived at the ranch, she'd tensed up every time he'd gotten close. He imagined most women would be apprehensive of a man they didn't know. More so Mariah, especially after their initial meeting and given the fact she was staying at his house. But he didn't want her fearing him.

What would she do if he kissed her? As if someone had physically slapped him, making him realize his train of thought, Jackson stepped back.

He had no right to consider such a thing. He didn't need a woman in his life, especially when he hadn't even been man enough to hold on to Misty.

The memory of his wife's cutting words the night she'd left him lanced his soul. "The whole world may idolize you for being a great athlete, but remember when you're lying in bed alone that you weren't man enough to keep me. My heart belongs to another—the man who'll raise your child instead of you."

Popular, successful and wealthy, yet his own wife—the woman carrying his baby—hadn't wanted him. Jackson sucked in a deep breath, forcing his self-pity away. He'd been down that road before, and it was filled with nothing but rugged potholes and heartbreaking dead ends.

God had come into his life and filled those fissures with His love and forgiveness. Jackson knew he'd made many mistakes as a husband, reveling in popularity and the adoration of his fans and his success more than in his wife's affections. The truth was he'd been immature, arrogant and selfish, never really concerning himself with Misty's needs—only his own.

He'd failed at marriage once and had paid a very high price. It had cost him his wife and the career he'd worked his whole life to achieve. He'd be stupid to make that mistake again. He had avoided women for the past six years, and at the first real test, here he was, swooning over the very reporter who could destroy the life he had built for Hailey and himself. Jackson moved back another step.

Mariah stared at Jackson. A humming security light near the barn, along with the starlight, barely illuminated his features. Features she was far too attracted to. Features now reflecting some inner struggle.

Had he been about to kiss her? She'd almost thrown her arms around him, but then he'd stepped away. If she stretched out her arms she could still touch him, but he suddenly seemed distant.

Was there something about her he didn't like? He'd said in his prayer he was attracted to her. Spinning back around, she allowed her gaze to latch on to the Big Dipper again. She sighed, forcing her thoughts off the man beside her.

She thought of earlier tonight. What would it be like to have a close-knit family like his? Even though he and his brother had disagreed about her coming, they'd been man enough to put their argument aside tonight and, in spite of the tension lately, had even joked some at supper.

"What's runnin' through that pretty head of yours?"

He thought she was pretty? Grateful for the darkness, Mariah touched her cheeks. Her face felt warm, like a flannel nightgown fresh out of a clothes dryer. She searched for a response she could voice out loud—something other than thoughts of the near-kiss—or rather, near miss—before he'd sidetracked her.

"I was thinking how close your family is and feeling a bit jealous."

"Yeah, they are a blessing."

She needed to keep focused on her story and not the alluring man sharing the porch. "So, you've lived here ever since you quit football?"

He exhaled a heavy sigh but didn't answer.

"I can see why you love it here. It's so peaceful...like no place I've ever been to."

The air smelled crisp and clear, with no hint of car fumes. Far off, a horse whinnied and another one answered. Somewhere to her right, an owl hooted in the dark night. She hugged her arms close to her body, missing the warmth of Texas.

"Yeah," he finally said, as if it took a huge effort. "I moved here right after Hailey was born. I didn't want her exposed to the relentless paparazzi I encountered in the football world, and I wanted her someplace she'd be safe."

"You think a ranch is a safe place for a young girl? Safer than the city?" Mariah remembered with frightening intensity the rattlesnake in the barn and Hailey on the ladder, only a few yards away from it.

"Safe enough. She knows what's allowed and what isn't and rarely disobeys."

The edge in his voice told her he didn't like her questioning his parenting skills. He was a good father—she'd give him that. She'd enjoyed watching the tickle fight in the living room earlier between him and Hailey. Jackson had obviously allowed his young daughter to win the silly game as both had wrestled to tickle the other's feet. A smile tilted her lips as she remembered watching Jackson laugh until tears swarmed in his blue eyes.

Remorse tamped down her lightheartedness. Had her father ever once played with her? Mariah searched the depths of her mind, unable to come up with a positive response. Her childhood had been the complete opposite of Hailey's.

She swallowed back the jealousy that threatened to choke her. If Jackson's God was so good, why had He allowed an innocent girl to lose her only loving parent at twelve years old—a girl on the verge of her emotional teenage years? Why did she have to care for an abusive alcoholic father and a cruel brother? Why had no man loved her enough to want to care for *her?* To protect her? The stars above blurred into swirling illuminations of light and darkness. If Jackson's God cared so much, why didn't He care for her?

She cleared her throat, fighting away the tightness. She struggled to regain her composure as courage and determination overcame doubt and self-pity.

She had a story to write. Her job depended on it. She didn't want to think about the other four articles she'd turned in—the ones her picky editor said were garbage and not worth wasting ink and paper on. This was her last chance.

If she didn't get this story—and make it a good one— she'd most likely be out of a job. And her deadline was looming closer. Jackson was a good guy—one she longed to get to know better, but she'd never been able to rely on a man. And if she didn't tread carefully and got too wound up in his troubles, she might end up deciding not to do her story at all—and then where would she be?

Distance.

That was what she needed.

It was time she headed to bed. As she stepped back, her oversize boot caught on a board. She flailed her arms as she struggled to regain her balance.

Faster than she could blink, Jackson grabbed her. He held her upright while she maneuvered her foot back into the boot, and then with the heave of a breath that warmed her cheek, he pulled her against his chest.

She was momentarily stunned, and her arms hung to her side as he crushed her against his solid chest. As if they had a will of their own, her arms slipped around his waist.

All her life, she'd longed for someone to love her. She knew it was too soon for Jackson to actually care for her, but here in the darkness, she could pretend for one moment that she meant a little something to him.

"Mariah." Jackson's voice was a velvet murmur. His hand moved up her back and cupped her head. His pounding heart echoed her own as her head rested against his chest, nestled in his tender grip. She'd never known such gentleness in a man. A strange excitement upset her normally balanced control.

"Mariah, I—" He loosened his grip and looked down at her. His hand slid through her hair until it rested against her cheek, warming it. His thumb brushed against her lip, sending swords of sensations warring with rapiers of guilt. Did Jackson actually feel something for her, or was he just lonely? Was she simply a convenient distraction to his humdrum existence?

Jackson tensed, and she sensed him battling his own struggles. Doubt squelched her growing feelings. She didn't want Jackson to like her merely because he was lonely. Mariah desperately needed to be cherished for who she was herself. Nobody except her mother had ever loved her—not even God, who her mother claimed loved her more than anything.

Mariah closed her eyes, as she sensed Jackson's face drawing closer. Her heart pulsated with a vengeance in her ears. A breath away, he paused—she knew because she could feel the gentle puffs of his coffee-scented breath on her face. What was he waiting for?

Cupping her cheeks, he brushed his thumb over her mouth again. Her trembling knees threatened to buckle.

Suddenly, an explosion shattered the quiet night with the roar of splintering wood and a brilliant light flashing near the road. Even from this distance, Mariah could hear the debris hitting the ground. Baron, locked in the barn for the night, barked frantically.

Mariah blinked. The bright glow hurt her eyes. Jackson jerked away, staring across the yard.

"What was that?" she cried.

"I don't know. There aren't any buildings that direction. Just the road."

He raced across the porch, his boots slamming against the wood as he ran down the steps. "Get inside! Lock the door till I come back."

"You're not going down there alone." Mariah released her white-knuckled grip on the porch rail and propelled her legs into motion. "I'm going with you."

EIGHT

"I don't have time to argue." Jackson pinned her with a stern look that he'd probably perfected on Hailey. "Whoever did this might still be down there. I've got to try and catch 'em."

The door opened, and Deuce rushed out, dressed in red plaid flannel pajamas. "What happened?"

"Don't know. I'm headed out to check. Keep the door locked." Jackson turned away.

"You can't go alone and unarmed." Mariah hurried down the porch steps.

"There's a rifle behind the seat in my truck."

"I'm going, too." She wasn't about to miss this scoop. Mariah shuffled across the gravel to Jackson's truck in the oversize boots.

He paused before opening her door. "I'd feel better if you were locked in the house, too."

Mariah hesitated for only a moment. She couldn't pass this up and shook her head.

Jackson sighed loudly and brushed an assortment of papers lying on the passenger side of the bench seat onto the floor and held out his hand, helping her up. She shut the door as he ran around the front of the truck. Like a moth drawn to a porch light, Mariah's gaze sought the glow that brightened the night sky like a house lit up with countless Christmas lights.

Jackson jumped in and had the truck racing down his driveway before she could get her seat belt fastened. The engine rumbled. Gravel popped and crunched beneath the tires. From the direction of the barn, Baron kept up his tirade.

She glanced at Jackson's profile, trying to ignore how much she'd enjoyed their time together on the porch. She couldn't understand with all her history how she could actually enjoy being held by a man. But Jackson was different. He had a quality about him that others didn't.

In less than a minute, they bumped across the cattle guard and onto the country road. About a city block away lay a smoldering rubble, scattered in all directions.

"My sign!" Jackson moaned. "What in the world happened?"

Looking through the eerie glow, Mariah remembered how the impressive wooden marquee announcing her arrival at Angelfire had brought her great relief the day she'd arrived. And what a nice sign—more like a billboard with a trio of galloping horses—it had been, gleaming with a fresh, well-maintained appearance. But now the shattered remains littered the road and ditch. What a shame. "Looks like a war zone."

"I don't believe this." He slammed his fist against the steering wheel.

Mariah jumped. She didn't fear much, but one thing that still made her tremble was a man's anger.

Leaving the motor running and headlights blazing, Jackson bolted out of his truck and slammed the door behind him. Not since the day she'd arrived had she seen him so angry.

She shivered, remembering her father's tirades.

Jackson yanked a board off the road and flung it into the

darkness beyond the remnants of smoldering debris. She could hardly blame him for being mad. Who wouldn't be at such senseless destruction? But with no one else around, she was Jackson's only avenue for venting his anger. Would he take his rage out on her? The memory of her father doing that very thing was still vivid in her mind. Maybe Jackson would only yell. Dare she risk finding out? She reached for the door handle but then paused.

No, she was letting her irrational fear of the past overwhelm her. Jackson didn't seem the kind of person to hit someone else. But then again, he was a man—and an athlete. She pressed her hand against her churning belly. Could she afford to give him the benefit of the doubt?

Fear for herself warred with concern for Jackson. This was stupid. She was totally overreacting. Sucking in several calming breaths, she focused on the smoldering debris. Who had done this to him? And why?

Too bad she didn't have her camera or cell phone. She watched him kick a couple of charred boards off the road, and then he marched toward the grassy shoulder and stomped out several small fires. The brief sprinkle earlier this evening must have helped contain the fires, because instead of spreading, the half dozen or so small flames seemed content to burn out once their source had been devoured.

Jackson stood in the middle of the road, his hands on his hips, his face turned upward. Was he praying again? Talking to God in that comfortable manner of his?

He turned and strode back to the vehicle. Anxiety twisted Mariah's insides like a swirling carnival ride, mixing with compassion for all he was enduring. He didn't deserve this.

Instead of getting in, Jackson walked past the driver's door to the rear of the truck. The bed tilted with his weight, and metal scraped against metal. Moments later, he passed in front of the headlights again, carrying a shovel. For the next several minutes, he shoveled dirt on the few remaining fires and flung the larger pieces of debris off the road. With the last of the flames fading, the area grew darker, illuminated only by the truck's headlights and the stars overhead.

Jackson looked around. Obviously satisfied, he turned and strode toward her. He tossed the shovel into the bed of the truck, sending a loud clatter echoing across the quiet night. Jackson slid inside, the heavy odor of smoke accompanying him, and he started the vehicle. He grasped the steering wheel with both hands and heaved a sigh. "This doesn't make any sense. Why would someone do this?"

He pounded the wheel again. When he turned to face her, Mariah all but melded with the door as she flashed back to her childhood years and how her drunken father had vented his anger on her. Jackson lifted his hand toward her. She flinched, eyes closed, waiting for the slap that always came when her father was angry. She saw her father stomp across the room, swing his arm and smack her so hard she fell against the scarred coffee table, hitting her shoulder.

Mariah jumped again when Jackson's hand brushed her shoulder. He gently touched the back of her head, and she jerked away, bumping the door. Her heart pounded a frenetic pace.

"Are you all right?" he asked, his voice kind and full of compassion.

He toyed with a strand of her hair. Exhaling her pent-up breath, she opened her eyes and peeked at him through the darkness. His strokes were gentle, not those of a raging beast.

"What's wrong, Mariah?"

Relief surged through her veins. He'd never had any intention of taking his frustration out on her. She'd completely misread the situation. Feeling guilty for putting Jackson in the same category as her father, she sucked in a steadying breath and willed her heart to stop its pounding.

Warmth from the heater saturated her feet as a blush warmed her cheeks. Suddenly thankful for the darkness, she tucked one leg under her and turned in Jackson's direction. Maybe Jackson needed some comfort.

"Seeing this upsets you." He blew out a loud sigh. "I knew I shouldn't have brought you."

"That's not what's bothering me."

Jackson's tense expression relaxed. "Care to share?"

She blew out a loud sigh. "I don't handle men's anger well."

He stroked her head. "I'm angry at this senseless destruction, but I'd never hurt you."

"I'm used to men who lash out when they're mad. My father was a cruel man who drank a lot. My brother is a lot like him."

Jackson turned to face her, his gut twisting. He'd had several football friends who drank, and he knew well how easy it was to lose control when they'd overindulged. He knew he was overstepping his bounds, but he had to know. "Did they hurt you?"

"Sometimes. My father got rough when he drank. He was never a kind man, and that only made things worse. Carlos—my brother—was a bully and pushed me around because he could."

No wonder she was so tenacious. No one had ever protected her, so she had to protect herself. "I'm sorry. No child should have to endure such a life."

"It is what it is." She turned to face him.

"I would never harm you. I hope you know that."

She nodded. "I do, and I'm sorry, Jackson. I'm really sorry about your sign. It was really nice."

He tugged her shoulders gently, and before she knew what had happened, she was seated next to him, wrapped in his arms.

"Thanks. I was rather partial to it." His warm breath

brushed against her cheek. "I've only had that sign a few months. Got it in August."

Mariah tried to ignore how Jackson's nuzzling her hair affected her equilibrium. Her hands began shaking, but not from fear this time.

"I just don't understand." He sighed against her head, and his breath smelled like peppermint, though his clothes carried the scent of wood smoke. "I mean, I don't have any enemies."

"I think you do. What about a disgruntled customer? Or someone you've wronged—recently or in the past? These attacks seem personal." She pressed her head into the hollow of his neck.

"Everyone knows I guarantee customer satisfaction. I've even taken back horses that people have had for several months and then decided they didn't want."

"That must hurt your pocketbook."

"Not really. I have a good reputation for quality, well-trained horses, and that's not something you can place a price tag on. It's worth taking back a horse now and then to keep people satisfied. Contented customers come back again and again."

Jackson tightened his grip on Mariah's shoulder. Another time, another place and this scene would have been romantic. A chilly winter's night, a myriad of stars illuminating the moonless sky, and a handsome man at her side. Still, her reporter's mind refused to take a backseat to romance.

"What about a disgruntled sports fan?" she asked.

"I'm sure there were plenty of those around when I left the Tornados in the middle of a winning season, but that was six years ago, and these problems only started recently."

Six years ago was when Hailey had been born. Had his wife's death at the same time of his daughter's birth been the full story of why he quit football? Her instincts told her there was more to the story.

"I guess we ought to be getting back. I've got the big stuff off the road, but I'll come down in the morning and clean up this mess."

Jackson shifted his long legs, and Mariah missed the warmth of his thigh resting against hers.

"Thank you for coming down here with me." His soft words sounded husky. "I'm not used to having someone share my problems—other than God, I mean."

Mariah turned her head to look up at him. With his arm still around her shoulders, he brushed back the hair from her face. "You're welcome," she whispered.

"Mariah…" Jackson's soft breath tickled her cheeks. His hand slid down the side of her face until his fingers brushed against her lips. "Your skin is so soft."

She held her breath as he continued to gently stroke her cheek. The longing to kiss this man ignited inside her with a passion she'd never experienced before. Rarely had a man ever gotten so close. What was happening to her?

Jackson leaned forward at the same time he nudged her toward him. His kiss was soft. Gentle. How could such a big, strong man be so tender?

Emotions stirred, she kissed him back, and he responded. All too soon, he pulled back, heaving a sigh.

"As much as I'd like to continue this, we need to get back to the house, and I need to call the sheriff and report this. I left in such a rush that my cell phone is at home." He placed a final kiss on her forehead then lifted his arm from around her shoulders and put the truck in gear. As she started to slide back across the seat, Jackson slung his arm around her again, pulling her against his side. "You stay put, you hear?"

Glancing up, Mariah could just make out a twinkle in his eyes. She nodded and then leaned her head on his arm, enjoying the sense of security she felt—something so un-expected. Something she'd never before experienced with a man.

Jackson tucked her head in the crook of his neck and rested his head against hers. In a jerky one-handed circle, he maneuvered the pickup in a one-eighty and drove up the drive.

She closed her eyes, daring to fantasize. What would it be like to live here as Jackson's wife and Hailey's mom? To be able to cuddle him every night?

Very nice. A wonderful dream.

Reality smacked her upside the head. It was not her dream to consider. She couldn't allow her growing attraction to Jackson to sidetrack her. Becoming a reporter had been her goal ever since she'd worked on the class newspaper in middle school.

As they pulled near the house, Mariah sat up straight. Allowing Jackson to kiss her had been a mistake. A very pleasant mistake, but one she couldn't allow to happen again. He was her assignment.

His arm loosened, and she put a few inches between them. With great effort, Mariah forced thoughts of that wonderful kiss from her mind. She needed to finish this article. She couldn't allow her attraction to Jackson to interfere. She had to squelch those feelings and focus on getting her story.

Jackson felt as though he ought to be taken out and shot. He'd been upset at the loss of his sign and had wanted comfort. He'd yielded to his manly impulses and kissed Mariah. And what a kiss it had been. His first in over six years.

Mariah had responded but then pulled away and acted as if nothing had happened. And nothing should have. Regret swirled around him with the force of an EF-5 tornado.

He shoved the truck into Park, exited the vehicle and helped Mariah out. He should have left her at the house instead of allowing her to go with him. Deuce's boots shuffled as Mariah made her way across the gravel drive. Was she upset with him?

He should never have hugged or kissed her. He unlocked the door and allowed her to enter first, determined to put her out of his mind and focus on the issue at hand. Who could hate him enough to blow up his sign? Other than Howard Stunkard, he drew a blank. Maybe it was time to have the sheriff give him a visit.

Jackson rubbed the back of his neck, realizing how exhausted he was. Life on a ranch was rarely easy, but it had been even more stressful the past few weeks. He needed to talk to the sheriff, but there really wasn't anything the man could do until daylight. He'd call first thing in the morning. He sat on the mud bench and tugged off his boots.

Deuce slipped into the mudroom. "You let her wear my boots?"

Jackson glanced up and shrugged. "Seemed like a good idea at the moment."

"So, what happened out there?"

"Someone blew up our sign."

"What!"

"Yep."

Exhausted, Jackson pushed off the bench and padded into the kitchen, hoping to see Mariah once more tonight, but she was already gone.

Jackson swigged down the last of his morning coffee and glanced at his watch. Eight-thirty. Mariah was sleeping in this morning. Course, they'd had a late night. The hour of three had passed on the clock before he'd finally drifted off to sleep. Visions of a man dressed in black, stalking around his ranch, kept forcing him out of bed to stare out his window.

And then there'd been the memories of sharing that kiss

with Mariah. As much as he wished he hadn't kissed her, he couldn't deny he'd enjoyed it. But even if he had to wear blinders, he was determined to ignore any spark of attraction to that reporter. He'd be polite and kind but would not show even the slightest hint of interest. He had to do that for only a few days, and she'd be gone.

At the door, he slipped on his jacket and hat and stepped out into the cold December morning. Pulling his fleece-lined leather gloves from his pocket, he studied the ranch yard. Not a thing looked out of place. Baron yipped a little bark then trotted over for his morning scratch. Justin must have come early and let the dog out of the barn. So far, the boy hadn't disappointed him, in spite of his rocky history.

Deuce's ancient Pinto hatchback was gone from its place behind the house as he'd expected. His old friend was off to have breakfast with a few of his war buddies at the senior citizens' home in Claremore before he attended church. Same thing he'd done every Sunday for as long as Jackson could remember.

He warmed up his truck then headed down the drive to check out the explosion damage in the light of day. Maybe he could find some clues for the sheriff.

As soon as he reached the road, he knew he wasn't alone. Mariah's lavender jacket stood out against the stark winter landscape like a grape in a bowl of oatmeal. How had she managed to sneak out of the house without him noticing?

He clenched his jaw. Didn't the woman have a lick of sense? She'd been shot at two days ago, and here she was, out on the road alone. Mariah didn't even turn as he pulled his truck off the road and parked. He watched her study the area. She resembled a hound dog on a scent. In deep concentration, she walked down the side of the road then stopped and stooped down, touching something in the dirt.

Intrigued, he slid from the truck and strode to her side.

With her lips in a tight line, she glanced up at him, then back to the ground. "Jackson, I think I've found something."

NINE

"Look. Tire tracks." Mariah pointed to the ground.

Jackson squatted beside her, and the heat of her denim-clad leg radiated out to warm his chilled thigh. Ignoring the reaction it caused in his traitorous heart, he studied the marks in the hardened dirt. Yep, definitely tire tracks. Zigzag tread marks had been formed in the mud alongside the road and had hardened solid overnight. Hope soared. Maybe he'd finally found the evidence needed to locate the person harassing him.

"Last night's sprinkle made the ground soft enough that whoever blew up your sign probably made these tracks." She looked at him with a spark of hope gleaming in her eyes.

"Maybe. Could just be someone who lives down the road slipped off the blacktop, though. Still, they look fairly fresh. The mud that pressed up into the treads is in good condition. Maintained its shape well."

"I don't think the ridges would be so sharp if these were old tread marks that had been rained on."

Jackson stood, and Mariah followed. "These are definitely recent tracks. Got a tape measure, by chance?"

He nodded and returned to his truck, rifled through his glove box and found what he was looking for. Returning to Mariah's side, he handed it to her.

She pulled out the tape strip and measured the width and length of the tread marks then released hold of the metal, and it whizzed back in with a snap as the end tab hit the base. "Thanks," she said, handing the tape measure back to him. She pulled her cell phone out of her coat pocket, typed on a yellow screen that resembled a notepad and then slipped it out of sight again.

Jackson wondered how much info about him and his ranch she had stored away in that little device. Had she been making notes all along, and he hadn't noticed because he'd been too enamored with her?

He shook the thoughts from his head. He had more important things to stew on than his infatuation with Mariah or even the interview.

Pieces of charred wood he'd missed last night still littered the highway. He needed to clear the road before someone had an accident. "Let's build a fence of sorts around the tracks so we can preserve them until the sheriff can get out here. I called him, but he's tied up on the far side of the county until this afternoon."

Mariah glanced up. "We're going to town?"

He nodded. "I always eat breakfast at Auntie's Café on Sunday mornings. Deuce is gone to eat with friends. I thought you might prefer breakfast out to instant oatmeal or a Pop-Tart." He grinned at the way her face scrunched up. He figured she'd never eaten a Pop-Tart before. She probably ate some kind of hoity-toity bran muffin with her caffe latte every morning. Or maybe she was one of those diet-conscious women who skipped breakfast altogether.

"Breakfast sounds good. I'm dying for a big, fat waffle smothered in maple syrup. Do they have those?" Her thin eyebrows darted upward, hope shining in her sparkling eyes.

What had happened to the cold Mariah who'd stomped

in the house after his kiss? In a way, he wished she were still here. She was so much easier to ignore than this one.

"Ah, yeah." He cleared his throat, hating the huskiness in his voice. Maybe it was the cold morning air making his throat constrict.

She looked around then back toward the house. "Are you sure you want to leave? I mean, do you think it's a good idea?"

He rubbed the back of his neck. "I wondered that, too, but I won't be made a prisoner in my own home—and I need to go to church, especially with all that's going on."

She stared at his pants, brow crinkled. "You wear jeans?"

Jackson grinned. "You've never been to a country church, have you?"

"No, and I didn't dress for it."

Jackson ran his gaze down the length of her body. "You look fine."

"Thanks." Her cheeks flushed even pinker than they already were from the chilly morning. "Let's hurry, then. I'm starved. Maybe I'll get some biscuits and gravy, too." Mariah broke eye contact and picked up the closest piece of charred sign and then set it alongside the tire tracks. Ironically, he read the blackened word *fire* on it. *Angelfire*.

As he walked back to the truck, he remembered the day Lance, Evan, Kelly and he had bumbled their way through mounting the sign. Evan had wanted to save money, so his brother had talked him into installing it themselves. Having plenty of money in his bank account, Jackson would rather have just paid the sign company to do the work, but Evan had challenged him to do it, and he hadn't wanted to wimp out. What a mistake! In the end, they'd had to hire Sam Hawkins to bring his mobile crane from Claremore just to lift up the heavy billboard.

That night after they'd doctored their blisters and put ointment on their strained muscles, they drove into town together and devoured rib-eye steaks at Marvin's. Jackson could hardly get out of bed the next morning. This time around, wimp or not, he'd put his foot down and let the sign company do the installation.

Still, looking back on it, the whole day had been fun as the three males had battled to outdo each other, while Kelly had whined about all the testosterone in the air. It was a good memory, but one he didn't care to repeat.

"What are you smiling at?" Mariah stopped in front of the truck.

Busted. He'd been walking down memory lane and ignoring her. He picked up the board nearest him and sent it sailing off the road like a square Frisbee. "Just thinking about the day we put the sign up."

"It must have been a nice memory, judging by the look on your face."

Jackson tossed another board into the ditch and kicked some more debris off the road. He grabbed a three-foot-long plank and laid it along the southern edge of the tire treads. Crossing the two-lane road, he kicked more of the charred remains into the ditch.

He sighed. There really wasn't all that much left for the sheriff to study for clues. It was probably a waste of the man's time to ask him to come out here again.

Jackson pulled off his hat and held it in front of him, folding back the brim. For the life of him, he hadn't been able to think of a single person who had it in for him. Howard Stunkard wasn't happy he wouldn't buy back the horse that he'd bought from one of Jackson's customers, but he couldn't imagine the man destroying property. The old coot was mostly bluster.

Westin was a small close-knit community that had rallied around him and his daughter when he came back from playing football. The simple country folk were excited to meet him and proud of his accomplishments but had allowed him to live a normal life. Most no longer saw him as a celebrity but rather a rancher with a young child.

He breathed a simple prayer for the protection of his family and property.

"You're going to ruin your hat if you keep that up."

Jackson glanced at his hands, which were twisting his hat close to death. Black marks from the ash on his gloves had stained the brim. He heaved a sigh. Guess he'd be buying a new one after all.

Mariah crossed the road and stopped in front of him, taking the hat from him. He watched her gently smooth out the dents and wrinkles, and then she glanced up at the top of his head.

The cool morning breeze lifted the strands of hair framing her pretty face. The forty-degree temperature had painted her cheeks a dark rose, which only added to her appeal.

An impish grin tilted her lips, and then she reached out and grabbed hold of his jacket, about chest high, and pulled him down. As he leaned in her direction, his heart stampeded. Was she going to kiss him?

What happened to his decision to ignore Mariah? It wouldn't work if she was going to come on to him. He hadn't planned for that scenario.

Help, Lord! Against his wishes, his eyes shut of their own accord. After a moment, Mariah released her grip on his jacket and moved her hand to his shoulder. He felt one of her arms brush against his ear, sending arcs of electricity sparking through his torso and short-circuiting his brain.

Instead of the warm lips he expected to brush his, he felt his hat slide back on top of his head. "There—that's better."

Jackson opened his eyes and found himself looking directly into Mariah's. Her wide, pleasing smile took away some of his disappointment at not receiving another of her soul-stirring kisses.

I'm playing with fire. He almost laughed at the irony

of that thought. He didn't want a woman in his life, but if by chance one came his way, she would be a woman who loved God with all her heart—a countrywoman. What he had was a reporter far too distracting, who could destroy the peaceful life he now lived. If only he could remember that then he could keep his distance.

Breaking eye contact, he straightened and glanced around the road. "Looks like we've done about as good a job as we can here. You ready to go get that breakfast?"

Mariah looked down at her hands. "Could I wash up first?"

"Yeah, sure." Jackson gave her a hesitant smile and opened the truck door for her.

As he trudged around to the driver's side, he contemplated how much power Mariah had—the power to destroy the life he'd made for himself and his daughter. He'd lived the life of a celebrity who couldn't leave his home without being bombarded by the paparazzi and crazed fans, and he didn't want to endure that again, nor did he want that for his daughter. He liked the simple, quiet life that he'd created before all the craziness started. Somehow he had to get back there.

"I'll take the waffle special," Mariah told Trudy, the owner of Auntie's Café.

"Bacon, sausage or ham?" The waitress scribbled the order on her pad of receipts.

"Bacon, please."

"Just give me the regular, Trudy." Jackson slid his menu to the edge of the table.

Mariah watched the stout older woman amble away. She realized that people from all over the room were gazing at her. Almost as one, they turned away, concentrating on their food. As she continued to study the quaint country café, she caught covert glances darting her way. She turned back toward Jackson and sipped her water, not liking being the center of attention.

"You're the biggest news in town. Well, that and what's happening at the ranch. The gossip mills are running rampant."

She studied his nonchalant expression.

"It's true." He shrugged and reached for the sugar container. The café had old-fashioned glass sugar dispensers topped with metal lids with a tiny pour flap on each table instead of the small packets she was so used to. Kernels of popcorn were mixed in with the sugar. At home, she used uncooked rice to keep her sugar and salt from clumping together because of the humidity.

The café buzzed with conversation. Silverware clinked against dishes. Every time she glanced up, someone was staring at her. Squirming in her red vinyl booth, she studied her fingernails. She needed to clip them tonight—and there was black under two nails, probably from the charred boards.

"Just ignore those folks. That's what I had to do when I first moved here."

"Was it hard?"

"What?" Jackson stopped stirring his coffee and looked up.

Mariah could understand why people would stare at him. She could barely keep from gawking herself. He had removed his hat when they'd entered the café and stuck it on the old-timey coatrack on the wall near the entrance. That dark swatch of rebellious hair flipped forward onto his forehead, which was a lighter shade than the rest of his tanned face. His dark blue eyes radiated curiosity, making her scramble to remember her question.

"Was what hard?" he offered.

"Um…you know, always being in the public eye. Always having people wanting to touch you and begging for your autograph."

He shrugged. "Nah. Back then I loved the attention. It fed my tiny ego."

"Tiny?" Mariah couldn't hold back the grin that tugged at her lips. In his football days, J. D. Durant had been a media hound, eating up the attention.

"Yeah. Just about this big." He held his thumb and forefinger an inch apart.

"Yeah, right. I did my research, Mr. Always-Gotta-Have-The-Spotlight-On-Me."

Mock horror engulfed Jackson's handsome face. He lifted his hand to his chest. "*Moi?* You dare slam your oh-so-magnificent host?"

"If the boot fits."

Amusement danced in Jackson's eyes, and he shrugged his broad shoulders. "Okay, so I liked being in the limelight. Most athletes do. But that was then. Now I value my privacy."

Mariah lifted her brows at his comment. "What made you change your mind so suddenly? Why did you walk away from your career and never look back?"

Jackson leaned back in the booth. He glanced around the room then looked over his shoulder as if he were about to share some deep dark secret.

Mariah bent forward, not sure if the swirling in her stomach was from the delicious scents floating around her or if it was eagerness to hear what he'd say.

Jackson fingered his coffee-cup handle. "I quit football when my wife died—the same day Hailey was born." He glanced up, and the normally self-confident cowboy looked more like a lost schoolboy. "I wanted her to live an ordinary life, where she could walk down the street and not have to dodge cameras every day. It's the same reason I don't like the idea of you doing a story on me."

She stared at the table as understanding warred with the need to complete her story. "It's my job."

"It's my life."

"So, we're still at an impasse?"

He shrugged.

Mariah swallowed her disappointment. She wanted to ask about his wife, but Trudy walked up, carrying plates laden with steaming, aromatic food on one arm.

The waitress started with the plate nearest her shoulder and set it in front of Jackson. Then she placed a white plate covered with the biggest waffle Mariah had ever seen in front of her. Lastly, she set a plate of scrambled eggs, buttery grits and three slices of bacon beside Mariah's waffle.

"We don't eat like birds out here." Trudy wore a smug grin as she walked away. Mariah looked at Jackson, who smiled as if he'd just won the Super Bowl.

"We can't have you wasting away before you go home."

"I'll never eat all of this." She buttered her waffle, sliced it and then poured warm maple syrup across the top. Her mouth watered in anticipation.

"You can have my bacon and grits," she said. "The waffle and egg are enough."

"Nah, you eat 'em. Might put some meat on those bones." He grinned at his pun. "Get it? Bacon. Meat on those bones?"

Mariah purposely groaned loud enough for him to hear. "That was bad." She stared at his overloaded plate, which held three scrambled eggs, hash browns, two biscuits and four slices of bacon, resting next to two link sausages. On the side was a soup bowl filled with steaming sausage gravy Trudy had brought by on her last trip past their table.

"No, really, I think you should eat the bacon. After all, you are making a hog of yourself." She waved her fork at his plate.

"Ha-ha." He gave a fake laugh at her pork pun. "I'm just a hardworking cowpoke who needs nourishment. Gotta keep up my strength." He grinned and flexed his arm, drawing her attention to the bulge of his biceps beneath his sleeve. His expression sobered. "Mind if I pray?"

Mariah shook her head and closed her eyes, mainly to stop from staring at Jackson. She enjoyed their comfortable bantering and the quiet blessing he mumbled. After Jackson said amen, she slipped a bite of waffle dripping in maple syrup into her mouth. "Mmm! This is yummy."

"Yep. Trudy makes the best waffles around."

"I'm serious about the bacon. Take some of the eggs, too. After all, you owe it to me."

His eyebrows lifted. "What do you mean?"

"This." She waved her fork in the air over her plates. "You could have warned me they served so much food."

"Doesn't seem like all that much to me. Just normal." He layered ketchup on his sausage, making it look like roadkill, and then stuffed half of one link into his mouth.

"What time is church?"

He glanced at his watch. "Forty-five minutes, but it's just around the corner."

"I'm still surprised you wanted to come to town."

"I can't let whoever is harassing me run my life. I have to trust God and entrust my daughter and the ranch into His hands. No matter how much I want to protect her and my property, ultimately, they are safest in God's hands."

Mariah marveled at his faith in God. Most men would barricade themselves and their families in their homes until their attacker had been found. Jackson chose to trust God and allow his daughter to live as normally as possible. Her admiration for the man rose more each day.

"I am thinking about leaving Hailey at Evan and Kelly's until things settle down, although she'll make a fuss, because of you and Lilly."

"You just said you weren't going to let what's happening change things."

"Maybe not for me, but I can't take a risk where Hailey is concerned. Even though I trust God to keep her safe, I'm still a father who worries about her. It doesn't hurt to play things smart and take precautions. The thing is, I don't know if she'd be better off away from the problems at the ranch or with me, where I can keep watch on her."

A grin tugged at his mouth. "She called me this morning, pleading to come home. I caved and told her she could come home after church."

Mariah smiled. "Good. I miss her." Her long, dark lashes touched her cheeks as she glanced down to slice her waffle. He forked some eggs into his mouth, wondering what it would be like to come home and find a pretty woman waiting for him. Someone to laugh with and someone to cuddle with on cold nights.

Mariah glanced up and caught him staring. The corners of her mouth turned up in an embarrassed grin and her cheeks flushed.

Jackson looked away, surprised at the rush of emotions her smile created. He hadn't realized how lonely he'd been until she'd come along. How could he fall for her so fast?

Back when he'd played football, he'd been a pro at keeping his heart safe while enjoying time with the many women he met—at least until Misty had sashayed her way into his life.

The first six months or so of married life had been great, but after Misty discovered she was pregnant and had to give up cheerleading for the Tornados, she had been unsettled and unhappy. It had thrown him for a loss, too. He wasn't ready to be a father. But then bam! Ready or not, he'd become a widower, a full-time dad and a former football star, all at the same time.

Mariah nudged her plate his way. "I can't eat any more."

Jackson eyeballed her half-eaten waffle. She'd taken only a few bites of her scrambled eggs. "How can you be full when you keep pinching off bits of my biscuit?"

Her cheeks darkened. "They are really good biscuits."

Hard footsteps clacked on the tile floor as a man lumbered toward them and stopped at their table. "I thought that was your truck out front, Durant."

Jackson looked up, cringing at the sound of the scratchy voice that continued to harass him. Howard Stunkard. The man had tracked him down. He drank the last of his coffee, dreading the confrontation that was sure to come.

TEN

"Hey, Howard. Can I help you with something?" As if Jackson didn't know.

Howard slammed his meaty fist on the table. Silverware bounced and clinked together. Mariah jumped, spilling coffee on her shirt. Grabbing her napkin, she mopped at the mess and gave Jackson a questioning look.

"You owe me, Durant."

The man simply wouldn't give up. "There's no call to make a scene, especially on Sunday." Jackson glanced past the heavy man in faded, tattered overalls and saw that everyone in the café was staring in wide-eyed curiosity. With great effort, he held back a groan. He didn't like the whole town knowing his business.

Howard leaned forward, both hands planted on the table. "I want the money you owe me." His gray eyes bulged. His breath heaved as if he'd just climbed to the top of Spencer Hill, the highest point in the area.

Mariah stared wide-eyed, glancing from his face to Howard's. Slipping from his seat, Jackson stood. He had a good half foot of height on Howard. Maybe that would intimidate the old coot. At least, Jackson could save face in front of his neighbors.

"You know I don't owe you any money. You bought that

gelding from Mike Allenby. Your deal was with him, not me." He'd never dealt with anyone so unreasonable before.

"You trained that beast."

Howard straightened, but Jackson still looked down on the man's yellow-gray comb-over. Did Howard think badgering would get him what he wanted? "And I sold him to Mike. The gelding was broken in real smooth. He was a good horse till you got ahold of him. I ought to buy him back just to save the poor beast from you."

Howard sputtered, but his eyes glinted with the victory he thought was close at hand. "So, you will?"

His manly pride didn't want to back down, but he had the horse to consider. It would be better cared for at his place. "All right, I'll give you one hundred dollars."

Howard's eyebrows dipped down into a V. "That's highway robbery. I paid eight hunnerd for that worthless gelding. I can get more than a hunnerd from the killers at the stockyard."

Heaving a sigh, Jackson had to acknowledge the truth in Howard's statement. The gelding was too good to be sent to the killers. "All right, four hundred. Take it or leave it. But I don't want to hear another word about it either way." Jackson crossed his arms over his chest and glared at the older man.

Howard mumbled and kicked the bottom of the booth, yanked a grimy red bandanna from his back pocket and swiped at his chubby face. "Might as well get a few hunnerd for the worthless creature, just to get him out of my barn, so's I don't have to feed him no more."

Jackson felt as if he'd won a battle. Actually, he had. Now maybe the guy would quit pestering him with all those phone calls. It was worth four hundred dollars to get Stunkard off his back.

As Jackson slid back into his booth, he glanced around the café. This was the first time he could remember it being so quiet in here. Gazes darted away from his, and the gentle murmur of conversation kicked back in. Several of his friends nodded, encouraging him that he'd done the right thing. Silverware clinked again. He looked up at Howard. "Bring the horse over tomorrow."

The man straightened as best as he could with that potbelly of his. "Fer that price, you come get 'im. And I'll take my money now."

Jackson shook his head. "You'll get your money when I get the horse."

Howard sputtered like an old truck trying to turn over its rusty motor, then pivoted and waddled toward the door. "What are y'all looking at?" he growled to the crowd as he exited the café.

"Wow! Do you get many customers like him?"

Jackson looked at Mariah. "He's not my customer. I'd never sell a horse to that man."

"So his first name's Howard. What's his last name?"

"Stunkard. Why?"

Mariah pulled her phone from her coat pocket, flipped it on, then made a notation.

"What are you typing?" He leaned forward but couldn't see the screen from where he was sitting.

"Uh…just a note. You know—a suspect list."

"You think Howard Stunkard could be doing all those things on the ranch?"

Mariah blinked, staring innocently at him. "Don't you? He certainly seems to have a vendetta against you."

Jackson shrugged. "Honestly, I don't think he's capable of masterminding something so elaborate. The man's just lookin' for some easy money. I don't know what Mike was thinking when he sold that horse to Howard." Running his hand through his hair, he glanced at his watch. "Time to get to church. I'm getting the better end of the deal anyway. That sorrel gelding's a good horse. I'll work with him a bit to settle him down, then turn around and sell him again. Or maybe I'll keep him. Ready to go?"

She nodded and slid to the end of her booth. Jackson stood. He pulled twenty dollars out of his wallet and laid it on the table, then offered her his hand and tugged Mariah to her feet. He gave Trudy a wave and headed for the door. Almost in unison, every head in the café turned in his direction again.

At the door, he paused and held up a finger to Mariah, signaling her to wait. Turning back to face the crowd, he scanned the room. "I know you all are dying to meet my guest. This here's Mariah Reyes, a reporter from Dallas."

Mariah's eyes widened, and then she looked at the floor. A dark rose stained her cheeks. When she didn't budge from the front door, he sidled up next to her, took her hand and tugged her to his side.

"She wrecked her car and is staying at the ranch till it gets fixed. Anybody got any questions?"

He could tell by their curious expressions that every one of them did, but he doubted anyone would voice them.

John Blanton slid out of his booth, surprising Jackson. "We all heard about your troubles, J.D., and want you to know if you need help, you can call any of us and we'll come runnin'."

Heads all around the café nodded, warming Jackson's chest. "I appreciate that."

Trudy marched forward and hugged Mariah, pulling her free from Jackson's grasp. "Welcome to Westin."

"Thank you."

As soon as the older woman let go, Mariah slipped around Jackson and scurried out the door. He nodded to the crowd, grabbed his hat off the rack and then followed her outside. His boots pounded out a quick rhythm on the sidewalk as he jogged to catch up. When he drew even, Mariah stopped fast and slugged him in the arm.

"Hey! What was that for?" He rubbed the sore spot where her fist had landed.

Crossing her arms, she scrunched up her face and scowled. "You embarrassed me half to death back there."

He hadn't meant to embarrass her. He'd thought it would make things easier for her if she'd already been introduced to a chunk of the town. Hat in hand, he twisted the brim.

"Never mind." She glanced up, wagging a finger in his face. "Just don't embarrass me in public again."

His mouth pulled into an ornery grin. "So, does that mean I can embarrass you in private?" He nudged her in the side with his hip.

"No!" She pinned him with a glare, but before she turned away, he saw her fighting a grin.

His grin faded as he opened the truck door. What would Mariah think of his simple church?

He muttered a prayer to God, thanking Him for protecting her from the shooter and for giving him a chance to get to know Mariah, even if he'd balked at first. Who could have thought a recluse would ever be attracted to a reporter?

God still worked in mysterious ways.

Sunday evening, Mariah stood at the mudroom door and watched Jackson and Justin at the corral. Ever since attending church this morning, she couldn't get the minister's message out of her mind. She'd never heard the Bible talked about in such an easy-to-understand manner. She had always thought of herself as a good person who tried to do what was right, but was she missing out on the wonderful gift God wished to give her? The gift of salvation?

"Missy, you mind telling everyone that supper's ready?" Deuce asked from the kitchen.

"Sure." She stepped out, and her gaze zipped to where Jackson leaned against the corral, watching Justin walk a black horse. He cut a nice figure with his broad shoulders, narrow waist and long-legged jeans that fit oh-so-nicely. As if he knew she was there, he turned and smiled.

"Deuce says supper is about ready."

He winked, sending her stomach into a tizzy. Warmth rose to her cheeks, and she hurried in the barn to find Hailey. She had to be more cautious where Jackson was concerned. She couldn't let her growing attraction to the man keep her from writing her story.

She opened Lilly's stall and leaned against the frame, watching Hailey brush the filly's coat. "I'm surprised she lets you do that."

"She doesn't hold very still, and sometimes she tries to eat the brush."

Mariah laughed. "You'd think she was a goat the way she likes nibbling at things."

"Yeah."

Baron barked, and Mariah looked toward the front of the barn. Justin led the black horse back to its stall.

Lilly leaned toward her and whickered. Mariah entered the stall, latched the gate and then scratched the little horse. Being around her no longer bothered Mariah, and she was proud that she'd overcome her fear. Maybe she'd even let Jackson talk her into riding one day.

Baron barked again, just outside the stall. He jumped up, putting his paws on the stall gate, and whined. Mariah shot him a look. "What's his problem?"

"He wants to play," Hailey said. "Let's go out and take Lilly for a walk."

"Deuce says dinner is ready. We need to go inside."

"Oh, phooey. I need to get Lilly's dinner first." The girl slipped from the stall, leaving Mariah alone with Lilly. Thankfully, Baron followed Hailey, whining all the way. Hailey returned with a huge bottle that sported the longest nipple Mariah had ever seen. Lilly nickered and hurried toward the girl.

"She's hungry, isn't she?" Hailey grinned.

Baron sat just outside the stall, barking harder. The black horse across the aisle, disturbed by the dog's barking, tossed his head and whinnied, moving restlessly in his stall.

"Hush, boy!" Hailey gave the dog a stern stare. "You'll scare Lilly."

Baron whined, but Mariah watched as the dog trotted outside. She started to turn back to Hailey, but a whiff of smoke snagged her attention. She looked where Justin had been, but he was gone. Surely he wasn't smoking in the barn, not with all of the hay scattered about. Still, the scent was so strong, she had to investigate. "Hold on a minute," she told Hailey. "Let me check on something."

She exited the stall, sniffing as she went, but as she neared the one Justin had been working in, the odor lessened. She noticed him outside, talking with Jackson—so where had the smoke smell come from? Turning toward the back of the barn, she headed for Lilly's stall, but a popping sound yanked her gaze to the rear doors. Mariah gasped. A haze of smoke rose up toward the loft. Flames licked at the wood along the bottom of the door. She had to get Hailey out!

The shrill beep of the smoke detectors thrust Mariah into motion. She ran to the stall. "Hailey, c'mon. We have to get out."

The girl stared up at the ceiling, her face white. She mouthed the word *fire*.

"Let's go. Now!"

Hailey's eyes widened, and she dropped the bottle. "We can't leave Lilly!"

"You go. Tell your dad. I'll get her."

Hailey took another look at the horse then raced out of the barn, meeting Jackson on his way in. "Daddy! Fire!"

"Go to the house and stay there," he ordered.

Baron's frantic barks continued. The dog had been trying to warn her. Mariah tugged on Lilly's leash, but instead of going forward, Lilly pulled back. "C'mon, girl. We've gotta get out of here."

She glanced at the back wall, and the flames were already higher. Suddenly, water showered down from above.

"Mariah!" Jackson cried, as he skidded to a stop outside the stall.

"I can't get Lilly to move."

"Go! I'll get her."

"But I promised—"

He frowned and yanked the lead rope from her hand then slapped Lilly on the rear end and yelled. The surprised horse bolted forward, out the gate and toward the exit. Jackson grabbed Mariah's arm and propelled her outside, at the same time Justin hurried out of the garage, pushing the motorcycle.

Jackson ran back into the barn and quickly returned leading the black horse. He passed the animal to Justin, who led it to the corral.

Deuce ran out of the house, waving. "I called the volunteer firefighters."

"Thanks! Keep Hailey inside." Jackson forked his fingers through his wet hair. "The sprinklers are working, but I don't know if it will be enough."

Mariah wanted to hold him—to soothe the ache she read in his eyes.

"At least all of the horses are safe. Good thing we put the other three out to pasture this morning." Justin shook his head, flinging water droplets.

"I feel so powerless just standing here." Jackson took a few steps toward the barn, but Mariah grabbed his sleeve. He looked in her direction, his eyes burning with anger.

"Don't. Hailey needs you."

His gaze shifted to the house. Hailey stood at the door, wiping her eyes. He jogged over to her, opened the screen door and lifted her up, cradling her in his arms. "Don't cry. Everything will be okay, pun'kin."

Justin suddenly made a mad dash back into the barn. Jackson yelled, but Justin didn't stop. He quickly stormed through the open doors again, carrying a pair of extinguishers. "Maybe we can work on the fire from the outside."

"Good idea." Jackson kissed Hailey and set her down. "Stay inside."

He strode over to Mariah, and Baron followed. He looked at the dog and held up his palm. Then he said, "Baron, stay!" Jackson caught Mariah's eye. "You stay put and keep Baron here."

She nodded. He squeezed her shoulder, giving her a tight-lipped smile, then spun and followed Justin to the back of the barn. Baron whined. Mariah stooped down and petted the dog, thinking how he'd tried to warn them. "Good boy."

Black smoke rose in swirls, but Mariah couldn't see any more flames. What a senseless thing to do. Anger battled pain. Anger at the person who set the fire, for she highly doubted it was an accident. Pain because this meant another loss for Jackson.

Lilly whinnied from the corral where she pranced back and forth. At least it was far enough from the barn that she and the other horse should be safe. Mariah took hold of Baron's collar. "C'mon, boy." He allowed her to lead him over to the corral. "Sit. Stay."

The dog obeyed, looking up at her as though he wondered how she knew dog commands. Mariah reached through the railings and smacked her lips together, making a kissing sound. Lilly trotted over and sniffed her hand. "Poor baby. I'm sure you miss your mama."

The similarities between her, Hailey and the horse jolted her. They were all motherless females. She blinked, startled by the sudden revelation.

At least Mariah had a few memories of her mother, but

Hailey had none, since her mother had died the night she was born. It made Mariah want to cry out to God, asking Him why He allowed mothers to die and young girls to be raised by fathers who didn't care. Instant remorse stabbed Mariah's conscience. Unlike her father, Jackson cared deeply for his daughter.

She was grateful that he had Hailey, because she would help him get through these hard times. She'd give him a reason to smile—laugh. And he had his siblings and friends— and his God. Mariah gazed Heavenward, realizing the sky had darkened, and the smoke now blended with the inky twilight. *God, if You're real, save Jackson's barn from total destruction. Lead the sheriff to the person behind all of this.*

An hour later, Mariah stepped outside and surveyed the scene. The stench of smoke still filled the air, but she was relieved to see the barn illuminated by the headlights of several vehicles. She desperately hoped the men had been able to save enough of it so that it wouldn't have to be torn down and rebuilt. Shadows cut through the lights, pulling her gaze to the men, where Jackson and Lance helped the volunteer firemen load their equipment into their truck. They waved as one of the trucks pulled out.

In the kitchen, Deuce rattled pans as he worked to prepare food for the men. She ought to see if she could help him, but first she needed to check on Hailey again. She went inside and padded to the living room. The girl lay on the couch, watching cartoons with Baron sleeping at her feet. Mariah would never look at that dog the same. If only she'd caught on to his warning sooner, maybe less of the barn would have been damaged.

She dropped down onto the couch, and Hailey smiled at her. "Are you doing okay, sweetie?"

The child leaned against her arm and nodded. She'd been unusually quiet since they'd come inside. Mariah hugged her, but her thoughts drifted back to the barn—and the person responsible. The footprints the men had found behind the barn could only have been made by a large man. Whoever it was had a lot of nerve, to set the fire when Jackson and Justin were on the other side of the structure. Had that been an effort to prove his power? Or did he know she was in the barn and had set the fire to harm her?

Her mind raced at the possibilities. Justin had been outside, but Jackson had been with him. Was it possible that he had run around back, set the fire, then hurried to the front again without being noticed? But later, he ran into the burning barn to get the fire extinguishers—maybe to make him look heroic? Was that his motive?

She tried to remember when Baron had first barked but couldn't determine if it was before or after Justin left. "Hailey, how long has Justin worked here?"

The girl shrugged. "Not too long. Since last summer maybe. Before that, he was in jail." Hailey turned back to her cartoons.

Mariah was surprised Hailey knew that bit of information.

After a few moments, Hailey glanced up at her, worry crinkling her brow. "How did the barn catch fire?"

Mariah's mind raced with thoughts of how to respond. "You'll need to ask your dad about that, sweetie, but it might be a good idea to wait until tomorrow." She checked the clock on the wall. "It's past your bedtime, and tomorrow is a school day. Time to get your jammies on."

"Okay. But will Daddy come and kiss me good-night?"

Mariah squeezed the girl's shoulder. "I doubt a herd of wild horses could keep him from doing that—after he gets cleaned up."

Hailey yawned and punched the remote, turning off the television. "I'm going to ask God again to make these bad things quit happening. Will you pray with me?"

Standing, Mariah nodded and tugged Hailey to her feet. A few days ago, she wouldn't have known how to answer that question, but now she did. "I'd be happy to."

ELEVEN

After the remaining volunteers had wolfed down hamburgers outside, Jackson shook the hands of each soot-covered neighbor who'd come to help fight the fire. "I don't know how to thank y'all."

Harley Barnes, the driver of the water truck that had made the difference in beating the blaze that had started to overpower the sprinklers when the water in the tank had run low, removed his helmet. "No need to thank us. You'd have done the same, I'm sure."

Lance leaned back against the corral, flicking soot off his jacket. "You sure cut a break, J.D."

Jackson nodded, glad his friend had seen the smoke and had come to help. "I thank God for enabling us to get the fire out so fast."

"Amen!" Jacob Linkwyler smiled. "Good thing you had the sense to build your barn with fire-retardant wood and installed that sprinkler system, or it would have been a total loss."

Several men grunted their agreement.

"I reckon we oughta head home." Delbert Mackey wiped his face with a handkerchief, leaving a trail of black along the cloth. "The wife always worries until I get back."

"Thanks again—and I mean it." Jackson gave the men a tight-lipped smile.

Evan, with Kelly in the passenger seat, drove around the volunteer firemen's trucks and parked. Both siblings stared at the barn for a long moment, then walked toward him as the last of the volunteers headed for their trucks.

Kelly smiled. "It's still standing. That's good, right?"

"How bad is the damage?" Evan halted next to Jackson, ignoring their sister. "Can it be fixed, or will it need to be torn down?"

"Don't know yet. The sheriff called and said to stay out until he can get an arson investigator over here." Jackson wrapped his arm around his sister when she sidled up beside him.

"I'm so sorry," she said. "It's such a nice barn."

"I'm hopeful that it can be repaired. I'm thankful the sprinklers and smoke detectors worked. And that Hailey and Mariah weren't injured." Or worse—but he couldn't voice that thought.

Evan's eyes widened. "They were in the barn when the fire started?"

Jackson nodded. "She and Hailey were caring for that filly we brought in from the pasture."

"How is my niece?" Kelly stepped away, looking up at him.

"She was shaken up and scared, but she's okay. Last time I checked on her, she was watching TV."

Kelly squeezed his arm. "I'll go peek in on her and see how she's doing."

"Deuce made burgers. There are some left, if you're hungry."

She nodded at him. When she opened the door, Baron bounded out. He trotted up to Jackson and licked his hand, skirted Evan and stopped in front of Lance, tail wagging. His friend pulled a dog biscuit from his pocket and tossed it for Baron to catch. The dog flopped down, chomping on his snack.

As soon as Kelly closed the door, Evan turned to Jackson. "You mentioned arson. So this wasn't an accident?"

"No. We found a discarded gas can out back. Someone set the fire deliberately." Jackson's gut lurched. He still couldn't believe someone hated him so much that they would endanger his daughter and Mariah.

"What are we going to do about these attacks?" Evan crossed his arms, staring at the barn. "This kind of stuff has got to stop."

"The sheriff thinks I should hire some men to guard the place. The county doesn't have enough money to pay for something like that."

"Might be a good idea. You gonna do it?" Lance asked.

"Maybe. But how would I even know where to station them? These assaults have been so random."

Evan shifted his gaze back to Jackson. "Did you find any other clues as to who did this?"

"Just a man's footprints."

Lance cleared his throat. "Makes sense that someone used an accelerant. How else could the fire have caught on so fast?"

"Yeah." Jackson heaved a sigh. He was tired and dirty. "I need a shower. Let's head inside."

"Yeah," they said in unison and turned toward the house.

Jackson took a final glance at the barn. *Thank You, Lord, for helping us get the fire out.* In the mudroom, he stripped down to his T-shirt and jeans. Lance, also in his undershirt, already had a plate, even though he'd just eaten outside. Evan was layering his burger with mayonnaise when Jackson entered the kitchen.

Kelly walked in. "Hailey is sleeping."

Mariah followed her but paused and leaned against the doorjamb, as if she wasn't yet comfortable around his family.

Except for Hailey, everyone he cared most for was in this

room. His siblings. Closest friends. And Mariah. He wasn't yet sure where, if at all, she fit into the picture. Kelly nudged him, and he realized he'd been staring. He glanced at his sister and had a sudden thought. Was she safe? What if his unknown attacker got tired of plaguing him and turned his wrath on his siblings?

"You stink, big brother." Kelly stepped away, but the gleam in her eyes told him she was halfway teasing.

"I know. I'm headed to the shower soon."

"Good idea." She plucked a pickle off the relish tray and popped it into her mouth.

Warmth flowed through him. His barn may have burned, but everything—everybody who really mattered—was safe. *Thank You, Lord.*

As he walked across the room, his gaze caught Mariah's. She stared at him for a long moment then stepped back to allow him to pass. He felt her following him and turned to face her when they were out of sight of the others. "Thank you for making sure Hailey got out of the barn so fast."

"Happy to do it." She looked up with concern in her gaze. "How are you?"

He shrugged. "Okay, I reckon. Things could have been much worse."

"True." She blew out a loud breath and narrowed her eyes. "I can't believe someone would set that fire when you were out front. It's almost like he was taunting you."

"I thought of that, too."

"How do we fight that?"

His eyes locked with hers, and he tried to ignore the way his stomach reacted to her use of *we*. "Only one way I know of—prayer."

She opened her mouth but then closed it and nodded. "I'm beginning to think you're right."

He ran his fingertips across her soft cheek. "God can fight

the unknown enemy in ways we can't begin to. Our job is to pray and trust Him."

Mariah paused at her bedroom door as Jackson continued down the hall. He had to be hurting, but he did a good job hiding his pain. She was getting too invested in his life—starting to care too much. If she didn't leave soon, she would lose her objectivity. Even now, she knew she could no longer write the story she had planned to. It wouldn't be fair to Jackson. He was a good man. He'd changed from the rambunctious rogue he'd once been and had matured into a responsible man and a loving father.

Her editor may not be happy, but her story would take a new angle.

As she walked into her bedroom, she considered his comment about God fighting unknown enemies. She hoped that was true, because if anyone needed a champion right now, it was Jackson. She longed for the faith he had—to believe that God really cared about her.

But she had cried out to Him earlier, and it looked as though the barn had been saved. Dare she believe God actually answered her prayer?

Monday afternoon, Mariah followed Jackson out to the barn to view the damage. She'd stayed in her room much of the day, trying to start her story but not having much luck. She thought of the article her boss wanted, but a much different one was forming in its place—one of a good man under attack. As they walked along the side of the barn, Mariah glanced at Jackson's hips. Today, he wore a holster and gun, reminding her of an Old West cowboy and that danger was never far away. He hadn't even wanted her coming outside alone. That both irritated her and made her feel protected.

The stench of smoke grew stronger as they stopped near the burned barn. Black scorch marks rose a good twelve feet off the ground. The door and the wood around them would have to be replaced, but most of the rest of the back side had fared pretty well. "It could have been a lot worse."

Jackson sighed. "I know. That sprinkler system and Justin's quick action to retrieve the extinguishers made the difference. But I can see now, though, that we need a backup water supply and even some sprinklers mounted on the outside eaves."

Mariah nibbled her lip as she remembered watching Justin charge back into the burning barn. "Do you think there's any chance Justin could be doing all of this?"

He spun to face her, his brows furrowed. "You suspect Justin?"

She shrugged one shoulder. "I did some research and found that he has a criminal record. He does seem rather rough around the edges. Though I can't come up with a motive as to why he'd do any of this."

Jackson's mouth cocked sideways, his irritation at her having researched and accused Justin evident. "That's because there isn't one. He's a good man who made some bad choices and is trying to turn his life around."

"Okay. Duly noted." She wasn't quite ready to mark him off her list of suspects, but he had moved down near the bottom.

"How did Hailey handle the news about her bodyguard?" she asked.

"I took Kelly's advice and didn't tell her. She thinks Ms. Garrett is a teacher's aide. But Hailey wasn't too happy when I informed her she had to stay in town all week. I finally decided that's the safest place for her as long as whoever is targeting me is still out there."

"What happens when Ms. Garrett goes home with Kelly and Hailey?"

He shrugged. "Kelly said she'd think up something to tell her."

Far in the distance, a bird screeched.

Jackson turned toward the sound and looked up. "That's an eagle's cry. They're fascinating birds. Did you know they mate for life?"

"Really?"

He nodded. "Yep. Pairs usually stay together until one of them dies. They even care for their young together. The father catches the prey and brings it back to the nest, where the mother tears it up and feeds it to her eaglets."

Mariah stepped closer. "I noticed the pictures of eagles in your office. Why are you so interested in them?"

"I studied them when I was a Boy Scout. They've always fascinated me." He shrugged and watched the bird. "They're so majestic, and there's a verse in *Isaiah* that says 'But those who hope in the Lord will renew their strength. They will soar on wings like eagles; they will run and not grow weary, they will walk and not faint.'"

She sighed. Wouldn't it be nice to have God renew her strength? There had been days when she thought nothing was worth the effort. That no one truly cared about her.

Jackson pulled off his hat and ran his fingers through his hair, drawing her out of her musing. She tried not to think of how much she would enjoy doing the same thing.

"Another interesting thing about eagles is they fly faster in turbulence than in calm weather. They glide on the wind currents and can even fly through the eye of a hurricane. God made them so that they can soar above the storms— even up to ten thousand feet high." He glanced at her. "Do you understand what I'm getting at?"

His passion for the topic pulled her in, but she didn't grasp his meaning. With reluctance, she shook her head.

He tilted his mouth in a beguiling manner. "Okay, how about this? We all go through troubles, right? Your car's wrecked, so you have to stay here until it's fixed. I have all kinds of strange problems now, right?"

She nodded, still not sure she was following him.

"Life's problems and temptations are like turbulent winds. They can sweep us away before we realize it and end up destroying us. Or we can catch the updrafts and ride out the storms of life with God's help. We don't have to go it alone. God will be the wind beneath our wings, if we let Him."

Jackson heaved a sigh. "I'm not too good at explaining things."

She laid a hand on his arm to encourage him. "No, I'm beginning to understand."

He flashed a smile that tickled her insides. "Whenever I have problems like I'm having on the ranch, I turn to God. He never promised we wouldn't have problems, but He's always there helping us through them. As I pray, I feel Him lifting me up above the circumstances, like an eagle soaring above the storms. The eagle can look down and see the storm. It's still there, but he's no longer buffeted by it. Same with us."

"That does makes sense."

"We can't outfly the storms in our lives, but they don't have to overwhelm us. By facing each problem that comes our way with God's help, we grow stronger. God is a loving God. He wants to help us. Eagles remind me of that."

He blew out a loud breath and kicked a rock, sending it skittering along the ground. "One day, when I was still playing pro ball, I got sick of all the pressures and expectations. I had money. Fame. Friends. But something was missing. I couldn't continue as I'd been going. I called Deuce—he worked for my uncle back then—and he explained my need for a savior. Shortly after Hailey and I moved here, he led me to the Lord. It's the best thing that ever happened to me."

Mariah lifted her gaze skyward. Way up through the bare branches of the trees, she could just make out the eagle as it glided across the cyan sky. It moved as if in slow motion. Hadn't so much of her life been in slow motion—at least until she got her job at the *Observer?* Now she rarely slowed down. Where would she be in two weeks if she didn't get her story? Back in Dallas and out of work?

If only she could have the faith in God that Jackson had, maybe her life would have more meaning. But the few times she'd attended church as an adult, the pastor had talked about God being a loving Heavenly Father, and she had left confused. The only model she'd had of a father had been a cruel monster.

But Jackson had given her the example she needed—of a dad who dearly loved his child and would do just about anything for her. If God loved Mariah only half as much, she wanted Him in her life.

Jackson watched Mariah from the corner of his eye. She looked troubled. He wanted so much to help her find the peace that he'd found. Life held little meaning without God in it. His certainly hadn't.

He turned back to the damage. Last night as he lay in bed, he'd gone over and over the scene, trying to remember if he'd seen anything—or anyone—just before the fire. Justin had been putting the gelding through some movements in the paddock and then took him to the barn. He had come out right afterward and hadn't gone around to the back of the barn. Could he have slipped out the back door and set the fire without Mariah seeing?

Jackson yanked off his hat and slapped it against his leg, receiving an odd look from Mariah.

"What's wrong?"

He scowled at her. "You've got me worrying about Justin now, when he's done nothing to deserve it."

"How can you be certain?"

"Because I've done nothing but help the kid. Gave him a job when no one else risked trying. He's grateful. Has told me more than once." He swung his hand at the charred wood. "He'd never do this. He loves horses—and cares about Hailey—too much."

"You may be right, but it's obvious that you can't be objective, so allow me. I can look at this situation with different eyes than you."

"And have you come up with anything?"

She was quiet a long moment then shook her head. "There hasn't been much evidence, and I can't find a reason why anyone would want to hurt you or your business."

He blew out a loud sigh. "Whoever did this had to be as tall as me, judging by the footprint."

"That rules out it being a woman."

He'd never considered that it might have been. She was right about her looking at the situation differently than him. He needed her help, but he didn't want it. Didn't want to be obligated to where he'd have to agree to the interview she wanted.

Several yards away, the few dead leaves of a small oak tree still clinging to their branches fluttered on the cool breeze. He wanted to trust Mariah. Trust that she would write a story that wouldn't share more than he was comfortable with, but she was a reporter—and reporters always wanted the nitty-gritty. The sensational story.

He'd never told a soul about the November night that Misty had died. About their stupid fight. After their senseless argument, he'd stood outside hollering at her, but the only sound he heard was clattering dead leaves rolling down the street in the brisk wind. Misty's taillights disappeared in the dark as she sped around the corner, tires squealing. She was leaving him for another man, even though their baby was due in a few weeks. The pain of her betrayal was still there, although it had lessened over time, but the nagging thought that he couldn't hold on to his wife still haunted him. If he'd been a Christian back then and more understanding and less demanding, would things have been different?

For years, he'd wondered who the man was who'd stolen his wife away. He'd probably never know. But in the end, they'd both lost, because Misty had crashed her car half an hour after she'd left him. She'd lived through the Cesarean but died shortly after.

He heaved a frustrated sigh, and Mariah glanced his direction. What did knowing who the other man was matter anyway? It was better to not know. At least this way he couldn't channel his hurt and anger toward a specific person. As long as he didn't think about those days too much, he was fine. Remembering the verse about taking every thought captive, he forced his mind to dwell on something else.

Shoving up his sleeve, he glanced at his watch. Two-thirty. Kelly would be picking Hailey up at school soon. He was anxious to hear how his daughter's day had gone.

Mariah glanced up, a gentle smile curving her lips. "Can we go inside the barn? I'd like to check on Lilly."

Jackson smiled. "That sure is a change from when you first arrived."

She shrugged, her cheeks turning wine-colored. "I know my fear of horses seems irrational to you, but I have never been around them before."

Reaching a hand toward her, he said, "I understand."

"Isn't that the house phone?"

Jackson cocked his head. "Yeah. If it's important, they'll call my cell. He wrapped his arm around Mariah's shoulders and led her around the barn again, enjoying the feel of her tucked up against his side. As much as he'd tried to fight it, he was falling for her.

But he wasn't sure she felt the same.

And what if she did?

Would he be man enough to keep her?

TWELVE

After checking on Lilly and looking over the damage to the inside of the barn, they drove out to the far pasture in the truck and checked the cattle and horses, which, much to his relief, had been okay. As Jackson parked the truck near the closed barn doors, he noticed Deuce's old car was gone. That was weird, since he usually took a short nap this time of day.

And where was Justin? Jackson looked around as he and Mariah walked toward the house. He should have returned by now from taking several bridles with worn leather to Jimbo McKenzie's for repair, but his car wasn't there, either. Since Justin had started working for him, he had been extremely reliable. Jackson's thoughts flicked back to Mariah questioning Justin's loyalty, but just as quickly, he shoved them aside. Maybe he'd left a message on the phone. He reached in his pocket for his cell, but it wasn't there.

The screen door screeched as he opened it, and he allowed Mariah to enter first. *Gotta oil that soon.* In the mudroom, he smacked his new hat against his leg to rid it of the dust it had collected then placed it on a hook. He shrugged off his long, black duster, hung it and then helped Mariah with her jacket. He walked into the kitchen, boots clunking on the tile floor. He stopped so quickly, she plowed into his back.

"Sorry. Why did you stop so fast?" She stepped around him and halted. "What happened here?"

The room looked as if a small tornado had blown through. Raw hamburger patties that Deuce must have prepared for supper sat on a tray on the counter. The kitchen reeked with the odor of partially sliced onions that sat on the cutting board. A can of soda pop sat on the counter, with glistening drops of condensation rolling down to form a puddle around its base.

Where was Deuce? His cook never ran off and left the kitchen looking like this. The man was meticulous to a fault. Mariah pulled a knife from the mayonnaise container, dropped it in the sink, then twisted the lid on the jar and put it in the refrigerator.

His gut tightened. "Something must have happened. Deuce would never leave things like this otherwise."

"I know. He amazes me with how clean he keeps his kitchen. Kind of puts me to shame." Mariah nibbled on her bottom lip. "Do you think maybe he ran to the store for something he needed for lunch?"

"He wouldn't go off in the middle of fixing a meal. It takes too long to get to town and back. I'd better call and see what's going on." Jackson picked up the cordless phone, noting the flashing red light that indicated he had a message. He punched in his phone number and password, while Mariah pulled a piece of plastic wrap out of a box and covered the onions. "You have nine messages," the recording said. Nine? That wasn't good. Something definitely had happened.

Anxiety wrapped around him like a boa constrictor, choking off his breath at the franticness in Kelly's voice. "Jackson, I—I can't find Hailey. C-call me."

His heart bucked. His gaze zipped across the room, verifying the time on the stove. School was well over, so she should be with Kelly now—and Ms. Garrett. Where was his little girl?

"What's wrong?" Mariah asked as she shoved the plastic-wrapped hamburgers into the refrigerator. She closed the door and hurried across the room, laying her hand on his arm. "Your face just went white."

Not responding, Jackson listened to the next message from Evan. "J.D., did you happen to come to town to get Hailey? Kelly's 'bout to have a heart attack. She picked her and the bodyguard up after school and then they went to the ice cream parlor for a snack, but now she can't find either one. You've got to let sis know if you have the munchkin. Kelly's freaking out." Evan's nearly calm voice indicated he wasn't too worried. He probably thought there was some kind of a mix-up. Jackson breathed a quick prayer, hoping that a misunderstanding was all that had happened. Had Ms. Garrett done something with Hailey? Had she felt threatened and hid his daughter? If so, why would she not have said something to Kelly?

He glanced at Mariah, his heart galloping ninety miles an hour. Worry tilted her eyebrows. She opened her mouth to say something, but he shook his head and punched the phone for the next message.

"Jackson, please." His throat thickened at the frantic plea in his sister's voice. "Tell me you've got Hailey. The whole town is looking for her. I'm getting scared."

He'd heard enough. Ignoring the other messages, he slammed the phone in its cradle and grabbed Mariah's hand. He snatched up his cell phone, which lay on the table where he'd eaten lunch. Of all the days to forget it. "Come on. We're going to town."

She tossed the dish towel in her other hand over a chair and hurried to keep up. "Jackson, what's going on?"

A muscle twitched in his jaw. "Hailey's missing."

"No! How could she go missing with Kelly and that bodyguard watching her? She's probably just playing with one of her friends."

"I pray that's what happened, but I've got a bad feeling in my gut about this." He shoved his hat on and grabbed his duster, not taking the time to put it on. Mariah stuffed her arms in her jacket as she followed him out the door.

In less than twelve minutes they made the normally twenty-minute drive to town. A crowd of people on foot and horseback gathered in front of the café. All eyes turned in his direction as Kelly spotted his truck and jogged toward him, with Evan and the sheriff close on her heels.

Kelly's anxious gaze scanned the inside of the vehicle as he pulled to a stop and quickly exited. "Tell me she's with you. You picked her up and just forgot to tell me, right?"

Jackson put his hand on her shoulder to brace her for his response. "No, sis, I didn't. I haven't seen Hailey since you took her home with you last night."

Kelly collapsed against him. "No! No." Behind her, Evan's face went pale.

As much as he wanted to comfort his sister, he needed action. His daughter—and her bodyguard—was missing.

Please, God, don't let that be true. There's got to be a miscommunication somewhere.

He eased Kelly away from him so he could look in her eyes. "Tell me what happened."

"After school we stopped at Carmichael's Ice Cream Parlor. I got to talking with Tammy Benson. Hailey had finished and said she had to use the restroom. Ms. Garrett followed her." Kelly sniffed, and Mariah handed her a tissue. "I thought she'd be safe with Ms. Garrett."

His sister glanced down at her feet then peeked up again with a look that made his blood run cold. "Hailey never came out, Jackson. I talked with Tammy for about five minutes. Then I realized neither Hailey nor Ms. Garrett had come back, so I went looking for them. I thought maybe Hailey was just playing with the water in the sink, like she does sometimes. But the bathroom was empty—and the back door was wide o-open—" Her voice cracked. Tears ran down her face and dripped onto her jacket. "They were both gone."

He closed his eyes, unable to look at the pain etched on his sister's face. Jackson felt a hand on his arm and knew Mariah was there, offering her silent support.

What do I do, Lord? Where's my daughter? Did Ms. Garrett take her—or has something happened to both of them?

"I'm so sorry, Jackson. What are we going to do?" Kelly moved away from him and leaned against Evan's arm then wiped her nose with the tissue.

"I've issued a BOLO," Sheriff Parker said.

"What's that?" Kelly asked. Evan wrapped an arm around her, and she cuddled into his side.

"A 'be on the lookout' bulletin. It's been sent to law-enforcement offices all over Northeastern Oklahoma." The sheriff turned back toward Jackson. "Kelly gave us Hailey's most recent school photo—the one that she carried in her purse—and a description of what your girl and Ms. Garrett were wearing at the time of their disappearance. I also checked, and Ms. Garrett's car is still parked at your brother and sister's house, so it's doubtful she kidnapped Hailey."

Jackson's gut twisted at the word *kidnapped.* He lifted his hat with a shaky hand and swiped the sweat pooling on his forehead in spite of the cool temperature. "Thanks, Todd. What else can we do?" Jackson clutched Mariah's hand, needing her quiet support.

"Have you called the FBI? Issued an Amber Alert? Or notified the NCIC?" Mariah asked.

Sheriff Parker nodded. "I called the FBI, but they will only come if we know Hailey was taken across state lines. The Amber Alert will go out just as soon as we've made sure Hailey isn't with any of her friends."

Fists on hips, Mariah marched forward, almost right in the sheriff's face. "But why wait? You're losing valuable time."

"There are standard protocols to follow. If Amber Alerts are issued too quickly and too often, people won't take them as seriously. Like crying wolf. Once I've determined that Hailey isn't with any of the people she knows, then I'll proceed with the alert."

Jackson pulled Mariah back to his side again and looked around at his friends. Most of the townsfolk had gathered in silent support. Trudy flashed him a smile that said "we'll get her back."

"Mariah mentioned something called the NCIS. What's that?" Evan asked.

"It's N-C-I-C. National Crime Information Center. They maintain missing-persons files," the sheriff responded. "And I've already reported her since there's no waiting period for that." He turned to Jackson. "Tell me everything you know about this Ms. Garrett."

Jackson started to respond, but all eyes shifted down Main Street as a black truck zoomed toward them and then suddenly skidded to a stop, slinging gravel onto the sidewalk in front of the barbershop. Lance plowed out of the cab and slammed his door. He marched toward Jackson with a determined look on his face. He grasped Jackson's shoulder and gave it a shake. "I just heard. We'll find her, J.D."

His friend's support meant more than Jackson could say. He nodded his appreciation, because he was certain his voice would crack if he spoke just then.

"Could she be with a friend? Or do you have reason to suspect someone…took her?" Lance asked, turning to the sheriff.

"She's not with a friend. I hired a bodyguard to protect her, and she wouldn't have allowed Hailey to go off with anyone. And she hasn't reported in—" Jackson's voice cracked.

Lance squeezed his shoulder in a reassuring gesture.

The sheriff cleared his throat. "We also discovered some physical evidence in the store."

A muscle ticked in Lance's jaw. "What kind of evidence?"

"I'm not at liberty to say. I'm waiting until a crime-scene analyst arrives from Tulsa. For now, I've got the area cordoned off." The sheriff looked over the crowd. "We need to organize search parties. We've covered the town once, but let's do it again. Pair off and expand the search to the outer edges of town. Check everything. Every nook. Every cranny. And nobody go off alone. We don't know if this was an isolated incident or not."

Jackson laid his head against the truck window. This couldn't be happening. Could someone have a vendetta against him so strong that they'd take his daughter?

His gut twisted. Was she cold? Hurt? Dead— No! He wouldn't think that. He'd search for her until he found her.

Hang on, baby. Daddy will find you.

Jackson looked at the blue sky. Just an hour ago things had been good, but now his daughter—the child he loved so much—was missing. His eyes burned. His heart ached. He needed the strength of his Father to endure this tragedy. He searched the Heavens as if he'd find an answer to his problem.

God, You've got to help me here. I don't know what to do. How to handle this. Protect my little girl. Help her to not be afraid. Help me, Lord.

Mariah watched Jackson. His heart had to be breaking, but so far, he'd been stoic. His head was tilted toward the sky, his brow crinkled from his unspoken struggle. Was he seeking guidance and strength from God?

She edged around Lance and moved to Jackson's side. He needed her. No, who was she kidding? She needed him—his steady strength. His immovable faith in God. Hailey wasn't even related to her, yet her own misery was so acute, it was a physical pain.

Jackson glanced down and then tugged her toward him. In that quick glimpse into his sapphire eyes, Mariah caught the shimmer of unshed tears. It was her undoing. She wrapped her arms around his waist and leaned against his chest, her tears soaking into his shirt. A tremble shook his body, matching her own.

"Shh. It'll be all right. We'll find her, honey," he said.

"I'm supposed to be consoling you," she mumbled into his flannel shirt.

Jackson leaned his head down. "You are. Just being here for me is a tremendous help." He pressed his lips against her temple, sending her emotions whirling.

She loved this man! When it had happened, she didn't know. Somehow, this gentle, steady man had slipped into her heart. She burrowed her face deeper into the strength of his chest and tightened her hold on him. If only she could protect him from the pain he must be feeling.

God, I've never put much stock in fathers, but if You're real, You've got to help Jackson find his daughter. If what he says about You is true, You can see all. You know where Hailey is. Protect her. Help her not to be afraid. Please keep her safe until we can find her. Please, God.

I don't deserve for You to answer my request, but Jackson is a good man. He loves You. He doesn't deserve the bad things that have happened, especially this.

"J.D., the detectives from Tulsa are here." Sheriff Parker lifted his hat and rubbed his bald head.

Jackson gently pushed her away from him, giving her a smile of gratitude. Taking her hand, as if he still drew strength from her nearness, he laced his fingers through hers and walked toward a sandy-blond-haired man. *Cocky* described him. He looked more like a California surfer dude than a lawman. Dark glasses covered his eyes and rested on a golden-brown face.

"I'm Riley Kincaid, from the Tulsa office. I was just on my way back from vacation, so I don't have much info on the case yet. You're the parents?"

Mariah's cheeks heated at his question. Jackson's lips tugged upward into a melancholy grin, and he hiked one eyebrow, looking at her. His brief smile warmed her heart.

"I'm the father. Jackson Durant. This is Mariah Reyes, a reporter from Dallas."

"Dallas?" Kincaid whistled through his teeth. He slipped off his sunglasses and eyed them with suspicion. "How did an out-of-state reporter get wind of this story so fast?"

"I was already here on assignment, covering another story," Mariah interjected, staring straight into his striking blue eyes.

He folded his glasses and stuck them in the inside pocket of his black leather jacket. His attire didn't hint at his job. Navy jeans hugged his solid legs and a light blue denim shirt emphasized his eyes.

"Is there somewhere we could talk more privately?"

"Let's go to the café," Sheriff Parker said. He pointed to Auntie's Café.

"Think we could get a booth in the corner, away from curious ears? I still haven't had lunch." The detective started for the café.

Mariah scowled at the man. How could he be thinking about food when a six-year-old girl was missing?

"It's a small town, but folks'll give us the privacy we need." Jackson followed, pulling her along beside him. She didn't understand how he could be so calm when she was aching to get out and pound the hills, looking for Hailey.

The townsfolk who had gathered nearby offered words

of encouragement as they walked away. Once they were seated in the back corner booth in the café and Detective Kincaid had placed his order with Trudy, he pulled a worn leather notebook from his jacket pocket. Was it just yesterday morning that she and Jackson had eaten a casual breakfast in this same restaurant?

"So, what's your relationship? You two seem rather tight."

Sheriff Parker, seated next to Kincaid, cleared his throat and looked to be fighting a grin. If the townsfolk had any doubts about their feelings for one another, they no longer did after Jackson's hug and kiss outside.

He stared at the sheriff for a moment, then glanced at her. What exactly was their relationship? She was interested in hearing his response.

"I suppose you know my history," he said.

Kincaid's eyes lit up and dimples in his cheeks made him even more charming. "Are you kidding? Played football myself in college—University of Oklahoma—'bout the same time your career was in full swing. What quarterback didn't dream of following in your footsteps?"

Irritated that he was talking sports instead of getting info on Hailey, Mariah chimed in, "Don't we have more important things to talk about than sports?"

Jackson squeezed her hand under the table and pulled it over so that it rested against his leg. "Mariah came to do a story on me for the *Dallas Observer*."

"I didn't think you did interviews anymore. Haven't read anything about you in years." Kincaid jotted something in his notebook.

"I don't normally, but my brother Evan thought we needed to promote our ranch and cooked up the idea. Kind of surprised me."

Kincaid eyed Mariah unabashedly. "Yeah, I can see why you'd be surprised—pleasantly surprised."

She felt torn between embarrassment, anger and pleasure that a man would think her pretty. But she didn't think Kincaid's comment pleased Jackson much.

"So, how are you going to help find my daughter?" His gaze challenged the lawman's.

"Another detective drove up and met me here—Sam Davidson. He's questioning people and checking to see if anybody knows anything. Have you noticed any strangers in town lately?"

"I talked to one yesterday," the sheriff said. "There were several others who stopped for gas, but nobody knows where they are now."

"Mariah is new to town, but she's been with me most of the time." Jackson pulled out his cell phone and glanced at it.

"She's staying with you?" A straw-colored eyebrow quirked up. He wrote something else in that book of his.

"She wrecked her car trying to avoid one of my horses that got spooked. Westin's a little town. There aren't any motels, in case you didn't notice. I let Ms. Reyes use my spare bedroom while her car is being repaired."

"Hmm."

Mariah wondered what Kincaid's "hmm" meant and why Jackson referred to her as Ms. Reyes.

"So, Durant, you got any enemies?"

THIRTEEN

Tired from answering the detective's questions and searching for Hailey for several hours, Mariah sat on the couch in Jackson's living room and stared at the orange flames flickering in the fireplace. Every fifteen seconds or so, the blur of Jackson's pacing body passed through her line of vision. His boots pounded out a dull rhythm, back and forth on the floor.

Her body cried for sleep, but her mind couldn't settle down any more than Jackson's could. Who had taken his sweet little girl? And why? Where was she now? There'd been no ransom note, even though the detectives had expected one.

They found out that Deuce had been doing some early supper prep when Kelly first called and told him about Hailey. He'd dropped everything, and along with Justin, he had gone into town to help in the search. After Jackson stopped by the house to see if Hailey had somehow made it home, Detective Kincaid had made them stay there in case a ransom call was received.

But that call never came.

Kincaid had said an estranged spouse was most frequently the one to abduct a child, but since there was no other parent, he was leaning toward either someone who recognized Jackson and wanted money from him or a random abduction by a stranger. No one could explain Ms. Garrett's absence—unless she'd been the one to take Hailey.

That thought made Mariah's blood run cold. Surely Jackson had checked her out before hiring her to watch his daughter. What if a stranger had grabbed Hailey and Ms. Garrett? Jackson's daughter was a beautiful, friendly child who had a smile for everyone. With people coming to the ranch all the time to buy horses, she was used to being around strangers. And the sheriff said there had been several in town today. His deputies were working on tracking them down. The one stranger who remained in town had been visiting friends and had an airtight alibi.

Weary, she looked up at Jackson as he passed in front of her again. His dark eyebrows scrunched into a straight line and his lips moved in a steady, silent prayer.

What did a man whose daughter had been kidnapped say to God? Why didn't Jackson throw something in rage and yell at the Man Upstairs for allowing this horrible thing to happen? How could he stay so calm—so composed?

The truth hit her hard.

Jackson's relationship with God was real. His God was real. And Jackson believed in Him with all his heart. The fact that his daughter was missing hadn't rattled his faith one iota. Mariah wanted that confident trust. Could she have the same connection with God that Jackson had? What was it he'd told her? Eagles fly above the storms. That was what Jackson was doing.

God, help me. Show me how to soar with the eagles—to fly above these troubles. I don't know what to do to help. Bring Hailey back home. Please.

Jackson kicked the leg of the coffee table, making her jump. "Waiting for a ransom call is a waste of time. I should be out there, looking for my daughter."

She stood and ran her hand down his arm. "I know it's

hard to wait. But driving around in the dark won't help you find Hailey."

"But just sitting here while she's out there somewhere, maybe hurt—or— It's driving me crazy."

"I know, but like you told me, you have to trust God to keep her safe."

He dropped onto the couch and ran his hands through his hair. "Will you pray with me, Mariah? Pray for Hailey?"

She wanted to tell him that she just had—in her own feeble way, but her throat had clogged with emotion. She nodded instead.

Jackson turned and slipped onto his knees beside her, and she knelt next to him, shoulder touching shoulder. He clasped her hand and bowed his head. For a long while, she could hear only a low rumbling coming from him— the murmur of a man talking with his God.

"Dear Lord," he finally whispered out loud, "we don't know why this awful thing has happened, but You do. You know where my daughter is. Keep her safe. Help her to not be afraid—" Jackson's voice broke. He tightened his grasp on her hand and pulled it against his chest, as if to draw in her strength.

Mariah clenched her eyes shut at the pain he was enduring. She wanted to take it all away. She didn't want this big, strong man to suffer. Maybe she could voice the words for him.

"God," Mariah began, "please take care of Hailey. Protect her. Keep her from being frightened. I remember hearing as a little girl when I went to church with my mom that You protect Your peo—" The warm drips of Jackson's tears on her hand were almost her undoing. He now held her hand with both of his and rested his chin against them.

Unable to continue, she grasped his hands. She cleared her throat and swallowed back the burning sting of her own tears. For a long time they knelt in silence. The scent of wood burning in the fireplace, along with its occasional popping and the house creaking when a gust of wind blew, made it almost seem like this was a normal night. But it was far from that.

Jackson's warm lips moved against her hand. Detective Kincaid's voice hummed as he talked on his cell phone in the kitchen, where he had set up his temporary headquarters, while Detective Davidson rested on Jackson's bed. Jackson had known he wouldn't sleep tonight and had offered his room to the detectives. Kelly attempted to sleep in Hailey's room, but she kept coming out every half hour to see if there was any news.

Mariah studied the dancing shadows on the Southwest design of the couch as the flames in the fireplace crackled and flickered. Her thoughts drifted back to her own needs. She desperately wanted someone to belong to. Someone who'd love her in spite of her too-quick temper and other shortcomings. Could God love her like that?

Jackson seemed convinced.

What did she have to lose?

Nothing really. Mariah leaned her head against Jackson's solid shoulder and closed her eyes. She wrestled with what to say, but then she focused on God and allowed the words to flow in her mind.

God, I need You in my life. I want You to be my friend and to help me through the hard times like You help Jackson. But even more, I need someone who can love me. Just as I am, with all my shortcomings. I've never known what it's like to have a real father.

Jackson lifted his head and rolled it back and forth, as if trying to get the kinks out of his neck. Standing, he tugged on her hand and gently pulled her up. For a long while he stared into her eyes, and then he gently ran the back of his forefinger down her cheek. "Thanks for praying with me.

You were a big encouragement. Your standing beside me today helped me make it through."

She felt her cheeks warming at his compliment. She had helped him? It touched her heart to think that maybe her presence had been a comfort rather than a hindrance.

The reflection of the fire danced in his eyes. Something else flickered there. Her chest tightened. Could he really care for her as much as she did for him?

Jackson leaned toward her, his eyelids closing. Warm lips gently touched hers. His kiss sent her heart soaring toward the sky. Wrapping his arms around her, he deepened the kiss, as if drawing in her strength. Too soon, he pulled back, his breathing heavier than before.

He rested his cheek against her forehead, and she nearly collapsed under the weight of his tired body. The man was exhausted but wouldn't give in to sleep.

"Does Hailey ever have trouble sleeping?"

"Why do you ask?" he said, his voice husky.

"Does she?" Mariah listened to Jackson's heart beating where her cheek now rested against his soft flannel shirt.

"Sure. When she was younger, thunderstorms scared her. I'd hold her in my arms in the recliner until she went to sleep." A gentle chuckle rumbled in his chest. "Sometimes I'd fall asleep, too, and we'd spend half the night there."

Mariah pushed away and took him by the hand. "Come on." She led him to his big recliner in the corner. "Sit," she ordered.

Jackson lifted his eyebrow with a flicker of amusement at her command. Then his shoulders sagged. "You know I can't sleep."

"Maybe you can't sleep, but you can at least relax and rest a bit. All your pacing is making me tired—and wearing out the floorboards. You need some rest if we're going to search tomorrow. Sit!" She crossed her arms, preparing for an argument.

He plowed his hand through his hair, leaving stiff tracks. Expelling a heavy sigh, he gave her a long stare, then flopped in the recliner and popped up the footrest.

"That's my boy."

An ornery smile tilted his lips. "Your boy?"

"I—" She didn't know what to say. When had she started thinking about him as belonging to her?

Jackson's hand snaked out and grabbed hers. He gave it a tug. She moved closer. He gave another tug until she was pressed up against the side of the chair.

His thumb rubbed back and forth on hers as he stared into her eyes, as if looking for something. "C'mere."

His next tug pulled her sideways and she fell against him. Stunned, she wasn't sure what to do, but she pushed up on the arm of the chair, and Jackson scooted over in the huge chair and helped her to get situated beside him.

He wrapped his arm around her. "If I have to rest, so do you." His gentle smile and the ache in his eyes were her undoing. Tears blurred her vision. Tears for Hailey. Tears for herself, because she'd be leaving soon and going back to Dallas. She cuddled in and rested her head against his cheek. For now, she'd hold him for as long as she could.

Because she loved him.

Jackson drove down the country road, dying a slow death. Hailey had been missing for twenty-four hours. He'd called the families of all her friends, but no one had seen her. Neither had anybody in town—at least not since she was taken. He swallowed the hard lump in his throat and blinked away tears. Visions of a vile man driving his frightened child farther and farther away from home assaulted him. If the captor had fled with Hailey when she'd first gone missing yesterday morning, they could be anywhere by now. Colorado. Florida. Maybe even—Mexico.

No! His grip on the steering wheel tightened. He couldn't

allow that kind of thought to take over. *Protect Hailey, Lord, and Ms. Garrett, wherever they are. Help me find them.*

Rubbing the back of his neck, he rolled his aching head back and forth. Against his wishes, he and Mariah were headed home again. Detective Kincaid insisted that he remain there in case they got a ransom call. But earlier this morning, he and Mariah had slipped away to attend a special prayer meeting at church while Detective Kincaid grabbed some sleep. Jackson had needed the support of his church family.

Glancing at Mariah, he wondered what she thought of the prayer time. Afterward, they'd joined one of the search teams until he'd received Kincaid's adamant call to return home. The way the townsfolk had rallied around him warmed his heart. Many friends and acquaintances, who were still helping with the search, had told them they were praying for him and Hailey.

The truck rumbled down the road. Jackson's gaze darted to Mariah. A smile tugged at his lips as he thought of how they'd shared the chair last night. It had been nice holding her—not being alone. But even with her comfort, he'd gotten only a few hours of sleep because he couldn't stop worrying about Hailey. He couldn't stand the thought of someone hurting her. He gripped the steering wheel so tight his knuckles turned white.

Mariah patted his arm and offered an encouraging smile, but he could see the worry in her gaze.

A light snow began to fall, so he flipped on his wipers. Was Hailey cold? Out in the elements? Was she still with Ms. Garrett? He gritted his teeth. He wanted to yell. Throw something. Never since he'd become a father had he felt so helpless.

He blew out a loud breath and glanced at Mariah. He needed to think of something else for a few moments or he'd go crazy. Her head rested against the side window as she stared out. He loved running his fingers through her silky hair. He loved how her dark eyes sparked when something irritated her. He admired her tenacious spirit and feisty temper. Her unwavering support since Hailey had gone missing. She was a beautiful woman, inside and out. But one huge thing stood between them—her story. What would she say if he asked her to not write it? Would she respect his wishes?

Mariah turned and looked at him, then glanced away. "Is there—uh—anywhere around here that we could stop soon?"

"We'll be back at the ranch in fifteen or twenty minutes."

She nibbled her lower lip, and her cheeks flamed. Her leg jiggled ninety miles an hour. "I really don't think I can wait that long."

He chuckled when she wouldn't look at him. She could barge her way in, like a big splinter under the skin, disrupting a man's life while researching her story, but talking about a natural thing like needing to go to the bathroom embarrassed her.

"We'll come to Lance's place soon. Will that work?"

"Yes, thanks." She glanced at him and flashed a shy smile. "Do you think we can get in? Lance was back at the search point when we left."

"Yeah, he never locks his door."

Jackson watched the trees and scenery blur by. He didn't want to mention what he'd found out this morning, but he had to. "I saw Tim Denton earlier. He said he made a drive to Tulsa yesterday and got the parts needed to fix your car. Should be ready by Thursday."

Mariah caught his gaze. "That's good, but I can't leave with Hailey missing."

Jackson nodded and swallowed several times to work the

tightness from his throat, hoping—praying—they'd find her today. "How's your…uh…story coming?"

She pinned him with another stare. "That's the last thing I'm worried about right now. Though I guess I'll have to work on it at some point, since my deadline's quickly approaching."

He drove the final few miles to Lance's house, contemplating what kind of story Mariah would write. What would her focus be? Would she tell the whole world where he lived now and thus open the gate for other snoopy media people to converge and destroy his peaceful life? He blew out a sigh.

Some peaceful world! Someone had already wrecked havoc on him. Blown up his sign. Set fire to his barn. Could the same person have taken his daughter? Or maybe it was more than one person. Could Ms. Garrett somehow be in cahoots with the kidnapper? He'd been given a glowing recommendation of the bodyguard by a close friend, so he didn't see how that was possible. He'd give up the whole ranch and walk away if it would bring Hailey back.

Who was after him?

And why?

He'd racked his brain trying to figure out who could hate him so much, but each time he drew a blank. It didn't make any sense.

He made the turn onto the gravel road that led to Lance's house. When was the last time he'd been here? A month? Two? Since Lance was at his house so often, he rarely needed to stop by his friend's place.

Lance had been a good buddy, even though he could be a grouchy bear at times. He'd changed a lot since their carefree days as football stars. Jackson had closely followed Lance's career during the years that his friend had remained in the NFL after he'd left. Jackson could remember sitting on the couch watching his old team while Hailey learned to walk and later when she sat on the floor and played with her dolls and plastic ponies.

The burning tightness in his throat threatened to strangle him again. *Oh, God, I don't know what to do. Where else to look. Where is she?*

Lance's clapboard house looked dingy compared to the crisp whiteness of the light snowfall. Trash, tools and pop cans littered the area. The place was more run-down than he'd seen it since Lance had started fixing it up. It was in worse shape than it had appeared to be a few days ago when he'd pointed it out to Mariah. Machine parts were scattered on the ground in the area in front of the barn where Lance was rebuilding a classic '66 Mustang in his spare time. Up close, he noticed that paint had chipped off the picket fence that encircled the front yard of the house, leaving it looking sad and neglected.

"It looks better from a distance," Mariah said. "Not really the kind of place you'd expect him to own."

"What kind of place do you think he'd buy?"

Mariah shrugged. "Oh, I don't know. He seems kind of flashy. I figured he'd live in a house that was as nice as that fancy car he drives."

"At least it has indoor plumbing." Flashing Mariah a teasing grin, Jackson put the truck in Park and turned off the motor.

Ignoring him, she opened her door and slid out. She walked around the front of the vehicle and wrapped her arms around her torso. "Do you think it's getting colder, or does it just feel that way because of the snow?"

He looked up at the gray sky, batting his eyes as snowflakes clung to his lashes. "I think maybe the wind has picked up. I sure hope Hailey…is someplace warm."

For a moment, he thought Mariah would burst into tears again. Instead, she made a valiant effort at blinking them back. He almost envied women that it was all right for them to cry.

They clomped up the three wooden steps to the porch, and then he twisted the knob and opened the door, allowing Mariah to go in first. It took a moment for his eyes to adjust to the dimness inside before he located the light switch and flipped it, illuminating the kitchen in a warm glow.

"Oh, my." Mariah lifted a hand to her mouth. "What a mess!"

Dirty dishes littered the countertops. Empty TV dinners coated with dried food and crushed soda-pop cans were scattered across the table and stove top. A distinctly sour odor attacked his nostrils.

"I'm almost afraid to see the bathroom."

He looked at Mariah. "Lance always was a bit of a slob, but this is something else. I've never seen it like this. He used to pay Kelly to come over and clean for him, but that didn't last long."

"I can see why if she had to deal with this all the time." Her lips tightened into a thin white line, and then she heaved a sigh. "Which way to the restroom?"

"Down the hall, first door on the right." Jackson walked to the window and stared out. *Please, God. Help me find my little girl. Keep her safe.*

A few minutes later, Mariah returned looking much relieved. Her gaze traveled over the kitchen, and she shuddered. "I was thinking of asking for a drink of water, but I'm afraid I might get salmonella poisoning or something."

"Try the fridge. Lance and I both got hooked on drinking bottled water because we traveled so much during our football years. You never knew what the local water would taste like."

Using only her thumb and index finger, Mariah carefully opened the refrigerator, as if scared she might contract a disease. Jackson smiled and shook his head. He walked around the table and took the bottle from Mariah's hands and opened it for her.

"Why, thank you, kind sir." Her teasing grin sent tingles of delight charging through him. She reclaimed the bottle, tilted it up and took a swig, the tender part of her neck moving as she swallowed. Lifting his hand, he ran his finger across it. Her skin was so soft. He loved to touch her. She stared at him wide-eyed and swallowed again.

Stepping closer, he pulled her into his arms. He'd decided that he wouldn't kiss her again, but he needed to feel her arms around him. There was truth in human touch being good for the soul.

Mariah melted against him as he laid his cheek on her head and held her for a few minutes. The old refrigerator hummed as the compressor kicked in, and the clock on the wall ticked off each second in a steady beat. Another second that Hailey was lost to him. How many seconds or minutes or hours would pass before she was returned?

He blinked his eyes as his gaze traveled over the littered cabinet. A box of Fruity Flakes sat open, next to a milk carton. His chest ached as if it were being squeezed with a vise grip. That was Hailey's favorite breakfast cereal. She loved the multicolored flakes and even used them for making decorations. Last year at Christmas, she'd meticulously picked out all the red and green flakes and glued them to a Popsicle-stick picture frame. After Deuce helped her glue a picture of herself to it, she gave it to Jackson for a Christmas present. It still sat on his desk. Funny, he never knew that Lance liked Fruity Flakes, too.

All of a sudden, Mariah went rigid. Her gasp penetrated the quiet and she pulled away. "Jackson, isn't that Hailey's coat?"

FOURTEEN

Jackson's gaze followed Mariah's finger to a blue denim jacket, lying on the floor under the table. His heart jolted. His mind raced. Wasn't that the coat Hailey was wearing when she disappeared?

"Why would Hailey's jacket be here?" Mariah voiced his unspoken thoughts. "Have you all visited here lately?"

Jackson shook his head. Maybe he was wrong. Hailey had several coats, and he'd never paid all that much attention to them. Kelly usually took Hailey shopping to buy clothes. "I guess she could have left it last time we were here, though I can't remember when that was."

She picked up the coat and studied it. "No, I'm sure I saw Hailey wearing this since I've been here. It looks like the one Kelly told the sheriff Hailey had on yesterday." Her face suddenly went pale as she reached in one of the pockets. She pulled her hand out and in her palm rested something long and purple. Mariah looked at him with a stunned expression.

He immediately recognized the four-inch-long purple flashlight. Along the side he read the inscription *Dallas Observer.* The night Mariah had arrived, he'd caught Hailey in her room after bedtime looking at a picture book by flashlight. That flashlight. The one Mariah had given to her only a few days ago.

His gaze lifted to Mariah's. His heart ricocheted in his chest. His mind swirled.

"This is the jacket Hailey was wearing when she disappeared. How in the world did it get here?"

She voiced his very thoughts. Suddenly, something that had been nagging at him made sense. He reached for his hat, yanked it off and smacked it against his leg. A fire burning deep within him threatened to ignite. Had he been duped by his best friend?

Jackson tugged his daughter's coat from Mariah's hand and sniffed Hailey's scent. His eyes watered, and he hugged the jacket to his chest. He didn't want to believe Lance would take his daughter, but the truth was staring him in the face. He cleared his throat. "Something's been bothering me. I've always taught Hailey to fight back hard if someone tried to kidnap her. I told her no matter what they said or did, she should scream her head off and kick and fight. We even practiced. I wondered how someone could take her and nobody heard a peep."

What if Lance had done something to Ms. Garrett and then tricked Hailey into going with him? Could his best friend have kidnapped his daughter? He pulled a chair out and all but melted into it. No!

"Would Hailey have gone willingly with Lance if he'd said the right thing?"

Jackson nodded. "It's the only thing that makes sense." He grabbed hold of an empty plastic cup on the table and squeezed so hard it cracked.

The idea that his supposed friend would abuse his relationship and steal his daughter sent an unstoppable rage building within him. Jackson growled and lurched up, lifted the edge of the table and sent it tumbling over with a loud racket that made Mariah jump.

She hurried to his side, grabbed his upper arms and forced him to look at her. "You have a right to be angry. There's no way you could have prepared for something like this. But we aren't even positive Lance's done anything. We need proof."

Jackson glared at her. He knew. Somehow he knew. Lance had always been jealous of his success and of his finding a woman to love when Lance couldn't. And Lance had taken several hard knocks lately with getting hurt and losing his mother.

"You don't suppose Hailey could be around here somewhere, do you?" Mariah squeezed the plastic water bottle in her hands. "Why would Lance be out helping to find her if he did something with Hailey? Unless—"

"It's his alibi." Jackson stared at her a moment then spun into motion. His daughter might be here! In this very house. "Hailey! Where are you, baby?"

He raced from room to room, calling out her name. Searching. Hunting. His lips moved in a steady prayer. "Please let her be okay. Help me find her, Lord."

He opened the closet doors in Lance's bedroom while Mariah searched the other room. Nothing. Just Lance's junk. More and more junk. He'd never noticed before how much of a slob his old friend was.

Friend. Ha! He'd have to stop thinking in those terms if Lance had anything to do with Hailey's disappearance. He still didn't want to believe it was possible.

Something skittered across his mind, and he struggled to grasp it. He'd always wondered how someone could get close enough to his barn to set it on fire without Baron barking. Could that be why Lance had fed Baron a biscuit every time he'd arrived at Jackson's house? He heaved a derisive snort. Had that been part of the man's plan? Make friends with Baron so he could move around and destroy Jackson's property without a peep from his dog?

He crossed the room, and his heart jumped. On the bed was a half-packed duffel bag. Lance's clothes had been tossed in haphazardly. He didn't remember Lance mentioning taking a trip.

"Jackson, you'd better come here."

His blood suddenly ran cold at the ominous tone of Mariah's voice. He rushed down the short hallway and into a surprisingly tidy bedroom. White-faced, Mariah looked up from the closet. Both of the sliding doors were open, revealing a four-foot-wide opening. On the closet walls were dozens of photos. Pictures of him and Lance in their glory days before they'd quit football—all with Jackson's face x-ed out. And there were more.

He rushed into the room to gain a full view of the closet, and his heart stopped. His blood ran cold. The wall was a giant collage of him, Misty and Hailey. There were several pictures of Kelly and even a few of Mariah.

She moved to his side. "This is creepy stuff."

He slipped his arm around her and pulled her close. Sweat ran down his temples, tickling his cheeks. His heart pounded out a frantic rhythm as he stared at photos he'd never seen before.

There were revealing pictures of Misty, which could only have been taken by someone she trusted. Someone she had been intimate with.

He closed his eyes, wanting to push the images away. Anger, disappointment and shock coursed through him like a turbulent river. Why hadn't he recognized the signs? Lance had always been quick to hug Misty and place a kiss on her cheek whenever he had seen her. Jackson had just thought it was his charming friend's way of greeting her. Not once had he considered that Lance might have been the man Misty was leaving him for.

Jackson curled his hand into a tight fist. He'd even let the guy date his little sister. How could he have been so blind? His gut swirled as he thought about Lance romancing his sister and—his wife.

"We've got to call Kincaid. He needs to see this." Mariah's words cut into his thoughts.

Jackson stepped forward and yanked off a picture of Misty in a revealing negligee. As he reached for a picture of him and Hailey horsing around near his barn, Mariah's hand on his arm stopped him.

"Don't. You're tampering with important evidence."

"This was my wife," he gritted out through his clenched teeth.

"I know, and I'm so sorry, Jackson. But you have to leave this alone until the authorities see it. It shows Lance's state of mind."

He sagged against her, needing her strength and support. "I never thought for a second that Lance was the man Misty loved. It never entered my mind. She was leaving me, you know. The night she was killed we had a terrible argument. She told me that she was in love with someone else. She was leaving, and the other man was going to raise my child. I can't tell you how that tore me up."

"I'm so sorry, Jackson. I didn't know."

"Nobody knew. Right after Misty's accident, the doctors did an emergency C-section in order to save Hailey's life. Misty was brain-dead and not expected to live. She didn't make it through the night. Unable to face my friends and the media, I took Hailey as soon as she could leave and disappeared."

Mariah tightened her grip on him, and he absorbed the comfort emanating from her. "That's such a sad story. I don't know how you endured it all."

"I don't think I could have, if it hadn't been for meeting God. He became my strength. And I had to live for my daughter."

"But I don't understand how Lance could so convincingly pretend to be your friend all these years. Why would he?"

"I don't know. I wish I did."

Underneath his duster, Mariah ran her hands up and down his back. "I'm so sorry, Jackson. I can't imagine what you must be feeling."

He didn't know what he was feeling, either. Hatred for Lance swelled within him. The man he'd thought was his best friend had stolen Jackson's wife, attempted to woo his sister and had now taken his daughter. *Why, God? Why did You let this happen?*

With his free hand, Jackson pulled out his cell phone and called Detective Kincaid and told him what they'd discovered. "You'll let Sheriff Parker know?" He nodded his head as Kincaid said yes, and then he turned off the phone and pocketed it.

"Kincaid will be here soon. He said to wait here until he arrives." He rested his chin on Mariah's head and stared out the window. The peaceful snowfall was such a contrast to his raging emotions.

He knew in his heart this wasn't God's doing. It was the hand of man. Lance, a man corrupted by selfishness and greed. A man who'd refused to accept Christ as his Savior. He'd talked to Lance many times about God, but Lance always resisted, making up some lame excuse why he didn't want to become a Christian. Jackson had thought if he prayed enough that, in time, Lance would see the light.

Jackson knew how Jesus must have felt at Judas's betrayal. Closing his eyes, he sought God for strength and the ability to forgive his enemy, just as the Bible instructed. It was a hard thing to do, and he wasn't sure if he could. He gazed at the pictures of his daughter again—pictures of her when she was small, others of her with him or Kelly and those with Sabrina and Lilly. Lance had been spying on them for years. He wanted to smash his fist into the man's face.

Please, Lord, show me where Hailey is. Keep her safe and help her to not be afraid.

A familiar bark drew his attention away from his prayers and out the window. A black-and-white dog raced by. Baron. Jackson slipped out of Mariah's arms and moved to the window just in time to see the dog shimmy through a hole under the side of the barn. Why would Baron be way over here at Lance's? And why would he want to get into Lance's barn so badly?

Hailey!

He spun around so fast he almost knocked Mariah over. "Call Kincaid. Tell him I think Hailey's in Lance's barn. Then call Sheriff Parker and tell him what we found. Ask him to take Lance into custody."

He raced out the bedroom door with Mariah close on his heels.

"Why do you think she's in the barn?"

"Baron just crawled in there," he called over his shoulder.

Adrenaline charged through him. His daughter was in Lance's barn! He could feel it. His boots smacked loudly on the wooden floor as he jogged down the hall. He jerked open the back door and raced outside. He moved as if in slow motion. He couldn't get there fast enough. Skidding to a stop on the thin layer of snow, he grabbed the handle and yanked. A new latch and lock had been installed. Frantic, he searched for something to break off the latch.

Nothing.

He hurried around the side of the building to examine the hole that Baron had crawled through. There was no way he'd fit through it. Even Mariah was too big.

Turning in a circle, he scanned the area, looking for something to use as leverage. His gaze fell on the barn's side window. He wiped off the snowflakes clinging to the frigid glass and peered inside. "Hailey! Can you hear me, baby?" His warm breath made a foggy circle on the pane.

Baron's excited bark echoed from inside. Jackson wiped

off the fog and stared hard but couldn't see anything in the dark interior. He realized then that he was staring at the back of a cabinet or some big wooden structure. Lance must have wanted to make sure nobody could break in.

"God, help me here. I've got to get inside."

His gaze landed on his truck. Yes! Fishing his keys out of his duster pocket, he raced around the wall, stopping at the barn doors. He peered through a crack but couldn't see his daughter. "Hailey, honey, it's Daddy. If you can hear me, move to the back of the barn right now and stay there."

He ran to his truck, climbed inside and shoved the key into the ignition. With the truck in Drive, he thrust his foot down on the gas pedal just as Mariah ran out of the house. The vehicle revved forward, motor growling, and he plowed into the double barn doors.

The nose of his truck smashed through with a metal-crunching screech. He shoved the gearshift into Reverse. Tires spun on the slick surface. Metal scraped and wood cracked as he gained traction and soared backward, sending debris flying.

Mariah was at his side as he climbed out of the vehicle. "They're on their way."

Nodding, he rummaged around behind his seat, pulled out a flashlight and then grabbed her hand. "Come on."

Ducking down, they entered the barn, carefully stepping over shattered pieces of wood. Baron appeared from nowhere and yipped a welcome. He brushed up against Jackson's leg and then raced back into the dark interior.

Jackson flicked on his flashlight. A glowing white beam illuminated the area. He ran the light over the length of the barn, but he saw nothing out of the ordinary.

His heart plummeted. He'd been certain Hailey was here.

FIFTEEN

Stepping farther into the barn, Jackson directed the beam into every nook and cranny. But there was no sign of Hailey. All he saw were tools, a riding lawn mower, the normal horse paraphernalia and Lance's black truck. Even Baron had disappeared from sight.

Mariah's ragged breathing echoed in his ears. She clung to his arm with a vengeance. "That truck—it looks like the one that almost ran me off the road."

"I wondered why I hadn't seen Lance driving it lately. He didn't want you to see him in it."

"He must have not wanted me to write your story. But why?"

Jackson started to answer but heard a whimper and scratching sound. He twisted around and shone the light to his left. His frustration mounted. Where was Baron? And his daughter?

"Hailey! Where are you?" He closed his eyes and listened closely for a response. "It's Daddy, sweetie."

Baron's sudden bark drew his attention to the far corner of the barn. They squeezed around the mud-covered truck.

"Look! There's a door." Mariah tugged on his arm until the flashlight shone against an open wooden door. It'd been so long since he'd been in Lance's barn that he'd forgotten about the small tack room.

Jackson opened the door and entered the room first, his large body filling up the small entrance. Bridles, halters and a rope hung on one wall. Two saddles sat on wooden racks on the other side.

"Move on in, Jackson. I can't see."

As he stepped forward so Mariah could enter behind him, the wood under his foot creaked and gave way a little. Suddenly, he spun around, nearly knocking Mariah over.

"Hey! What's wrong?" Mariah swung her arms, fighting to not fall backward out the door.

He steadied her with one hand, reached around her and flipped on the light. A single bulb illuminated the room in an eerie glow. Jackson turned again and stooped down. At his feet was a door in the floor, made from evenly spaced slats with hinges on the left side.

A locked door. One he'd never seen before. The wood still emanated its fresh pine scent and had not faded in color.

Mariah leaned down. "That looks new."

"Yeah." In the corner nearest his left foot, several slats were broken, leaving a ten-inch hole. It looked as if an animal had clawed at the wood until it broke. Pieces of black-and-white fur were stuck in the cracked edges of several slats. His heart jolted. This must be where Baron went. He whistled and received a bark in reply.

"Was that Baron?" Mariah asked, pressing against his back and looking over his shoulder.

"Yeah. There must be an underground room."

"Well, hurry up. Open it."

Jackson was almost afraid to. If Hailey was down in that hole, she hadn't responded to his call. He didn't think he could handle it if his daughter was...dead.

He muttered another prayer for strength. It was time for him to fly above the storms. God would give him the grace he needed for whatever he would find.

Placing his forefinger and thumb in his mouth, he blew out a shrill whistle. From underground, he heard a bark. In a matter of seconds, Baron's wet black nose poked up through the hole, followed by his furry head. He let out a little whine then disappeared down the hole again.

Frantic, Jackson scanned the room for something he could use to break open the door. His gaze landed on a toolbox in the corner on a shelf. He flipped it open. A hammer rested on top of a conglomeration of tools.

Kneeling, he used the teeth of the hammer and worked at the latch. He pushed hard and one corner of the metal latch squeaked upward. Tucking the hammer in deeper, he leveraged his full weight and pushed on the handle. With a screeching groan, the small square end of the silver latch popped up. He tossed aside the hammer and lifted the door.

Jackson leaned it against the wall, and Mariah shone the flashlight down into the hole, revealing a dusty stairway. Rather than being cold and damp as he'd expected, a warm breeze whooshed upward. His heart pounded. What would he find down there?

He looked at Mariah and saw concern in her eyes. "You wait here. We don't know what's down there." If things were bad, he didn't want her seeing it and having to remember it the rest of her life.

"Nuh-uh, no way. I'm going with you."

Jackson took a step down. "Stay!"

"Don't forget, I'm a newspaper reporter, not your dog. I've seen a few things in my day."

Unwilling to waste any more time arguing, he took the flashlight from Mariah and directed the light on the dirt steps. He hurried down. The farther he went, the warmer it got. Instead of finding a dirty basement, Jackson was surprised to discover a small drywalled room—a fairly warm room.

The bottom of the steps made a sharp right turn and

continued down farther. His gaze landed on a square of
light flickering in the back corner of the room. A television? His heart jumped from his chest to his throat when
the flashlight beam illuminated what looked like a little
bed in the corner.

His blood ran cold.

Baron whined and lifted his head off the cot, tail wagging. Behind the dog was a small lump under a Tinker
Bell blanket.

Jackson's gut tightened. He tried to call out his daughter's name, but his throat was too thick with emotion.

"It's a room." Mariah stated the obvious as she caught
up with him.

"Here, hold this," he managed to croak out as he handed
the flashlight back to her. "Point it at the bed."

"Bed?" Mariah squeezed around him and gasped. She
took the light and directed the beam to the lump.

"Down, Baron," Jackson ordered.

The dog whined and moved to the foot of the child-size
cot but didn't obey. Jackson bent over and reached out with
a trembling hand, lifting the old blanket. He tossed it aside.

Mariah gasped.

Hailey lay huddled in a fetal position with her back to
him, her hands under her cheek, looking small and vulnerable. The muted sound of the television echoed from
the headphones covering her ears. Hailey wasn't moving.

"No. Oh, Jackson," Mariah cried, grabbing hold of his
shoulder. The flashlight bobbed up and down as her hand
shook.

Tears blurred his vision. Had God led him this far only to
be too late to save his child? The bed groaned and squeaked
as he lowered his trembling body onto it. Slowly, he reached
out and smoothed Hailey's hair off her face.

Warm! Her skin was warm! "Thank You, Lord."

"Is she—alive?" Mariah moved in closer and shone the light on Hailey's pale face.

"Yes." Jackson removed the headphones and gently shook her slim shoulder. When she didn't move, he rolled her over. Hailey scrunched her eyes together, obviously not used to the bright light, and she stretched. Suddenly, she opened her eyes and blinked several times. She lifted her hand and covered her eyes.

"Lance? Is it safe to go home yet?"

"Hailey, it's Daddy."

Hailey's little body bolted upright. "Daddy!"

Jackson pulled her slight form against his chest and wrapped his arms around her. "Oh, baby. I've been looking everywhere for you." Tears freely fell down his cheeks and into Hailey's hair. Mariah ran her hand down Hailey's head and then against his cheek before it came to rest on his shoulder. She was there again, offering her silent support.

"I missed you, Daddy." Hailey tightened her grip on his shirt. "Lance said a bad man was after you and me. He hid me down here so the bad man wouldn't find me, but I was worried about you."

Jackson glanced up at Mariah. In the muted darkness he could see her eyes widen. She stared at him with incredulity.

"Let's get you out of here, baby."

"Lance said I had to use headphones when I watched TV so the bad man wouldn't hear me. I was real quiet. He said the bad man hurt Ms. Garrett. Did they catch him yet?" Hailey pushed back and looked up into his face with childish innocence.

"I'm not sure, baby, but I hope so." His gaze roved his daughter's face. She looked just fine, except for the layer of dirt and the food stains around her mouth.

"I'm hungry. I had Fruity Flakes for breakfast and some cookies for a snack. But now I'm really hungry. Can I have a cheeseburger?" Hailey leaned her head against his chest again and yawned. Emotion swelled within him. Moments ago, he'd thought he'd lost her and now his precious child wanted a cheeseburger.

"Of course you can, pun'kin." *Thank You, God!*

He lifted Hailey in his arms and stood. It felt so good to hold her. To know she was safe again.

"Who's holding the flashlight?" Hailey asked.

"It's me, sweetie."

"Mariah!" Hailey lunged out of his arms and into Mariah's. "I missed you, too."

The light wobbled as Mariah made a frantic grab for his daughter. As she clasped her arms around the child, the flashlight slipped from her hand and sailed across the room. It crunched against the wall, sending them into darkness, except for the flicker of the tiny nine-inch television.

"Oops." Mariah giggled. "I missed you so much, sweetie."

Not quite ready to be free of his child yet, Jackson retrieved her and the blanket. "Let's get out of here."

"Sounds good to me," Mariah said.

They stomped back upstairs to the front of the barn. The closer to the door they got, the colder the air became. Jackson was thankful that Lance had at least seen to Hailey's comfort and told her a story so that she wouldn't be too scared. The little space heater downstairs had kept the room plenty warm. And she hadn't seemed the least bit afraid of the darkness. That amazed him.

In the sunlight shining through the big opening his truck had made at the front of the barn, Jackson set Hailey down and knelt beside her. Baron cuddled up against his leg, wearing a proud dog smile, and Jackson reached down and petted him. "You did good, boy."

Jackson's gaze traveled the length of his daughter's body. She yawned and looked up at him and grinned. "I'm happy the bad man didn't get you, Daddy. I prayed he wouldn't."

Jackson's throat tightened again. Here they'd been, frantically petitioning God for her safe return, while she'd been praying for them.

Hailey gasped suddenly. "Guess what! I asked God to send someone to stay with me because I was scared, and then Baron found me. Do you think God sent him?"

Jackson glanced up at Mariah, who smiled and shrugged. "I reckon He could if He wanted to."

Hailey squatted and patted Baron on the head. The dog licked her hand. "Cool. You're really special, Baron."

Jackson wasn't quite ready to relegate saint status to his ornery border collie, but he was ever so grateful that God had used the animal to comfort Hailey.

"If God can use donkeys and eagles to speak to people, why not dogs?" Mariah's profound statement surprised him.

Jackson wrapped the blanket around his daughter, and then he stood, lifting Hailey up again. She bumped his cowboy hat, nearly knocking it off. "Yeah." He grinned, tapping it down. "Why not dogs?"

Mariah watched father and daughter. Hailey planted a kiss on Jackson's stubbly cheek. "You need to shave, Daddy. You feel like a Porky Pig."

Jackson's laughter echoed through the barn. "You mean a porcupine?"

"Yeah," Hailey said. "One of those spiky animals."

"You mean prickly?"

"Yeah, that."

"You don't like prickles?"

Hailey's giggle warmed Mariah's heart. "No."

"Well, what about this?" Jackson ducked his head and rubbed his chin on Hailey's tummy.

She squealed, pushing at her father's head. "Stop! Daddy, stop." Her giggles filled the barn with brightness, almost as if someone had turned on a light.

Mariah hugged herself. How had she come to love this

family so quickly? And even more, how could she leave them? They'd woven their way into her heart like a fast-growing vine.

And God had answered her prayer. Hailey had been found. Safe. And He had even sent a furry guardian to watch over her.

Now she had a bargain to keep with God. And she meant to keep her word. As soon as she got back home, she would start looking for a church to attend.

"Let's get this munchkin home. She needs a bath."

"Can I have a bubble bath?"

"Bubble bath. Cheeseburger. Whatever you want, precious."

Mariah saw the spark in the young girl's eyes. "So, can I have my horse now?"

Jackson grinned but growled out, "Don't push your luck."

Yep, life was almost back to normal. And she had a story to write. Just which story? That was the question.

Jackson hugged Hailey again. If only Mariah's own father had loved her so much.

"What happened to the doors?" Hailey asked, staring at the gap in the barn.

"We had trouble getting in to you, baby. I had to use my truck to break in."

"Lance is gonna be mad."

As if the words were prophetic, tires flung gravel and a blast of gunfire ricocheted through the air as Lance's car raced toward them. The wood closest to Jackson's head exploded. Hailey screamed. Mariah dived for cover. In one smooth move, Jackson ducked, pressing Hailey's head against his shoulder, and backed up. Baron's frantic barks echoed through the barn. Jackson's concerned gaze locked with Mariah's.

"You're not getting out of there alive," Lance yelled in

a cold, hard voice. "I tried to warn that reporter when I ran her off the road, but she didn't take the hint."

So Lance *was* the one. Mariah's heart raced. How could they defend themselves against a gun? If only Jackson hadn't removed his for the prayer time at church and left it in the truck.

Jackson shuffled toward her and thrust Hailey into her arms. "You two get back down in the basement. Now!"

Hugging the girl, Mariah stared at him. How could she leave him alone to fight a madman? What if he didn't make it? She couldn't stand the thought.

Jackson must have been thinking the same, because he held her gaze. Suddenly, he reached out and pulled her and Hailey against him in a fierce bear hug. "I love you," he whispered in her ear. He gave her a quick peck on her temple then gently pushed her toward the back of the barn.

Mariah and Hailey hurried down the dark steps. Thankfully, the TV still cast out a faint glow, illuminating her way. "Sit on the bed, sweetie." Hailey obeyed and Baron jumped up beside her.

Mariah turned toward the stairs. "Don't leave me alone." Hailey's pleading voice cut right to her heart.

Mariah searched her pocket for her phone. "I'm not leaving you. I just want to check on your dad. Plus, I need you to keep Baron down here so he doesn't get hurt. Can you do that for me?"

"Why did Lance shoot at Daddy? They're friends."

Mariah sighed, all the time listening for sounds upstairs. What could she say to a six-year-old to make her understand? "Has Baron ever gotten sick and had to go to the doggie doctor?"

"Yeah, the vet," Hailey said in a mature tone.

Of course, a ranch girl would know what a vet was. "Well, Lance is sick. He needs a doctor to help him."

"You mean, kind of like when an animal gets rabies and goes crazy?"

This little girl was way too smart. "Yes. Exactly. Lance has kind of gone crazy and needs a doctor to help him."

"I'll pray for him. God will help."

Mariah longed to have Hailey's simple childlike faith. If God got them out of this situation unscathed, she was definitely going to learn more about Him.

"So, you'll keep Baron here while I go upstairs and see what's happening?"

"Yeah."

"Promise? In fact, why don't you put on the headphones and watch one of those cartoon videos."

"I already watched all of them—over and over."

She had to distract the child. "How about playing a game on my phone?" She punched the phone on and was glad to see it light up.

Hailey nodded and reached for it. Mariah watched her slide the pages of apps until she found a game she liked and started playing. Baron yawned and put his head in the girl's lap. Perfect!

Mariah trotted up the stairs and breathed a quick prayer. "Please, God, protect us. Get us out of this safely." She peered out the tack-room door and heard someone yelling. Jackson.

"I don't understand, Lance. I thought we were friends." He was hunched down behind the big riding mower, looking outside.

"Ha! You're so naive, J.D."

Mariah slipped out of the tack room and scooted past the truck and into a stall, her heart pounding like a jackhammer.

"You never even knew that Misty and I were playing around behind your back. The great Jackson Durant, star quarterback of the Texas Tornados. You could zigzag out of tackles all day but couldn't hang on to your own wife."

Mariah saw Jackson's shoulders sag. The arrow had hit its mark. Her heart felt as if it would crack open. So, it was Lance who'd stolen Misty's affections, just like he'd stolen Hailey. Mariah had suspected as much when she'd seen some of the risqué photos in the closet. What a foolish woman Misty must have been to choose a man like Lance over Jackson.

"But why now? Why are you doing this after six years?" Jackson's voice sounded husky. Mariah wanted so badly to go to him—to touch him. To offer comfort, knowing how much he must be hurting. But she needed to make sure Hailey didn't come upstairs.

"I tried to forget what you did for four long years. But the team was never the same after you left. You're the reason I don't have a Super Bowl ring. If you'd only finished out that season instead of running off after Misty died, we'd have won the play-offs and the Super Bowl."

"You don't know that for sure," Jackson hollered back.

"We were undefeated. We were the best. At least until you walked away, leaving us all high and dry."

Jackson eased his head up over the top of the mower. A gunshot burst past and shattered several panes of an old window that leaned against the barn wall. Mariah squealed and covered her mouth.

Jackson looked over his shoulder at her and scowled. He swung his arm in the air and mouthed, "Get down."

"And you're the reason Misty died. You took her from me. That hurt worse than anything else." Lance fired off another shot as if to emphasize his point. "When I first came here, I thought maybe I'd get even by taking Kelly away from you. Oh, I gave it a good try, but she was too immature."

Jackson clenched and unclenched his fist. Mariah worried he'd do something rash. How much could one man take before he exploded? *Help him, God.*

"When I got hurt, I lost my advertising contract, which bankrupted me. I'm losing everything while you just keep getting more and more."

"Things aren't important—people are. I cared for you."

"And that only made things worse. You never cared about being rich, but I did. That story the reporter planned to write would only help you."

"I don't see it that way." Jackson cleared his throat. "Why take Hailey?"

"The older she gets, the more she resembles Misty. You stole Misty from me, so I decided to let you know how it feels to have the one you love most yanked from your life. *I* was supposed to be Hailey's dad, you know. Misty wanted me to raise her, not you."

Jackson swallowed the knot building in his throat. "And what about Ms. Garrett?"

"Casualty of war. She got in the way, so I had to get rid of her. Just like I plan to do with you."

SIXTEEN

Jackson needed a plan. Somehow he had to get out of the barn and draw the fire away from Mariah and Hailey. He scanned the barn's interior. There was no rear exit, and the only window was blocked.

To his left, a five-inch section of window not covered by the cabinet revealed jagged shards of glass framing the hole made by a bullet. Even if he could clear the window of enough glass that he could crawl out, the noise would surely attract Lance before he could finish the task.

"I'd planned on taking Hailey and hightailing it out of here—just as soon as I'd thrown you off the trail by helping with the search," Lance hollered. "I never figured you'd come here to look for her. We're supposed to be friends."

Jackson snorted his indignation. "You've got an odd idea of friendship. Destroying property. Burning my barn. Stealing my daughter."

"She was supposed to be *my* daughter. She even looks more like me than you."

For a brief second, a horrible thought unlike anything he'd ever experienced rattled his whole being. Was it possible that Lance was Hailey's biological father?

No!

Jackson sagged against a hay bale, battered, as if he'd been sucked up inside a tornado. His arms shook and the strength fled from his legs. If Lance and Misty's affair had gone on for very long, it could be possible. After all, Hailey favored her mother and didn't look much like him.

God, how much more can I take? Please tell me it's not true.

He'd love Hailey like his own, no matter if he wasn't her biological dad, but he had to know the truth. "Just how long did your thing with my wife last?"

"Long enough. Doesn't take much time to fall in love with a woman as beautiful as her. It only took me a couple of months of listening to Misty's stories of how you didn't really love her, how football was more important than she was, to realize I wanted to help her. And I would have if you hadn't killed her."

Lance's accusation hit its mark, and Jackson winced. He hadn't been a good husband to Misty, but he'd had no part in her death. "I didn't kill her. She died in a car accident."

A couple of months, Lance had said. Relief flooded Jackson. Lance couldn't be Hailey's father, then. *Thank You, Lord, for that.*

Jackson inhaled a strengthening breath. He couldn't stay here all day and do nothing. Peering around the bale, he saw Lance pacing alongside his truck. Forward. Back. Forward. Jackson glanced at Mariah to make sure she was still out of the line of fire. Worry was etched on her pretty features. He had to do something to save his daughter and the woman he'd come to love.

He waited for the moment when Lance turned and paced away. Muscles coiled, he leaped forward, running hunched over to the front of the barn, just to the right of the opening made by his truck. Mariah's loud gasp echoed in his ears.

He peeked through a crack in the wall. Lance was on his forward pace now. He stopped and pointed the rifle toward the barn. The loathsome expression on his face looked nothing like the man Jackson had considered his best friend.

"You still killed her. You were so caught up in your career that you ignored her. She'd have been better off if you'd never married her."

Jackson wanted to respond that Lance was right, but he didn't want to give away his new position. In truth, he probably shouldn't have married Misty. They had both been too self-centered. Too demanding. Each wanting things their own way. But if he hadn't married, then he wouldn't have Hailey.

The bright flash of a reflection darted through the crack in the wall. Jackson peered out. A solid black SUV raced up the driveway. Lance spun around, facing the vehicle.

Recognizing his opportunity, Jackson ducked through the opening and dashed forth like a quarterback with the football charging for the goal line. Adrenaline surged, spurring him faster. Lance pivoted and raised the rifle.

Jackson took a flying leap. Lance fired, sending a bullet whizzing in the air. Behind him he heard Mariah's scream. Jackson plowed into Lance and grabbed hold of the rifle as they collided hard against the ground. Lance forced him over and sat on him, still wrestling for the weapon. Pale blue eyes, cold as the Arctic, impaled Jackson. Lance's face contorted into something evil as he forced the rifle toward Jackson's throat. "Should have done you in a long time ago," he ground out through clenched teeth.

Suddenly, gunfire echoed, jolting them both. Lance glanced up and froze.

"Hold it right there. This fight's over." With great relief, Jackson recognized Riley Kincaid's voice. Still, he kept a tight hold on the rifle, pushing it upward while Lance was distracted.

Lance glared at Jackson, breath heaving from their brawl. Jackson could see in his eyes that Lance wasn't ready to give up. He'd known him long enough to know he wouldn't go down without a fight.

With a fierce growl, sounding something like a savage beast, Lance yanked the rifle from Jackson's grasp. He jumped up, spun and aimed it directly toward the barn. Toward Mariah, who stood just outside the barn with a shovel in her hands.

"No!" Jackson yelled. He pushed up from the ground, as if in slow motion.

Gunfire rent the air. Lance jerked and turned backed toward Jackson, pain and confusion etched on his face. A growing circle of crimson stained his left shoulder. He dropped to his knees, dropped the rifle, then fell on the ground. Detective Kincaid rushed forward and kicked the weapon away from Lance's reach. Detective Davidson hustled past Jackson, pulled out his handcuffs and snapped them onto Lance's wrists. A dark red spot also covered the back of Lance's shirt where the detective's bullet had hit its mark.

Jackson's gaze rushed past them to Mariah. Thank God! She looked fine. Real fine.

She threw aside the shovel and jogged toward him, relief evident on her pretty face. He wrapped her in his arms, ever so thankful for the positive outcome of the day's events. "Hailey still downstairs?"

Mariah nodded.

"What was the shovel for?" he whispered in her ear.

"I was just about to rescue you when Detective Kincaid showed up."

Jackson grinned against her hair. He could see Mariah as a warrior princess rushing out of the barn in her lavender jacket, shovel held high to rescue her man.

Thursday morning, Mariah wiped off the fog her breath made on the kitchen window and stared at her partially repaired Mustang. Tim Denton had been able to get it drivable, but it would need bodywork once she got back home.

A wealth of emotions surged through her. Thankfulness that neither Hailey nor Jackson had been injured in the ordeal with Lance. Gratitude that her story was finished and that she was certain her boss would be pleased and her job secure. But most of all, she'd met the Lord. And her life would never be the same.

And then there was Jackson. Where did he fit in the scope of things? When she'd pulled into Angelfire's driveway a week ago, she'd never dreamed how much her life would change. All because of one man—and his God.

But Jackson hadn't repeated his words of love since the one time in Lance's barn. She understood since getting Hailey back he'd concentrated on his child and making sure she was okay, as he should have, but she hadn't expected him to grow more distant from her. She missed the closeness they'd shared.

"That was Howard Stunkard on the phone just now." Jackson stepped up behind her, his voice low. "He wanted to tell me how glad he was that Hailey was okay. And to wait a few days till things settled down before coming to pick up the gelding. Funny, he's the last person I expected to be concerned for Hailey."

She didn't turn, afraid that he'd see the emotions she was trying so hard to hold back. Whenever she thought of leaving, tears burned her eyes. Jackson heaved a loud sigh that tickled her hair. "I talked to the sheriff while you were packing. They…uh…found Ms. Garrett's body in the trunk of Lance's Camaro, and it turns out the tire treads we found down by the Angelfire sign matched the ones on Lance's car. The detectives feel certain that forensics will prove the bullet found out by the creek was from the rifle Lance shot at us. Looks like he will be going to prison for the rest of his life—if he doesn't get the death penalty."

"I'm sorry, Jackson. I know he was your friend."

"Yeah. I'm sorry, too."

The mudroom door squeaked open, and Deuce and Justin walked in. The old man's frizzy hair had been tossed around by the stiff breeze outside, making him look like Albert Einstein. Justin tugged off his hat and stood there studying the floor. Mariah wondered how she could have suspected the shy young man to be involved with the problems at the ranch.

"I'm gonna miss you, missy." Deuce shuffled across the room and enveloped her in a big, bone-crunching hug.

Mariah battled tears again. This old man had become like a loving grandfather to her. "Same here."

He took her by the shoulders. "Anytime you're in our neck of the woods, you stop by, and I'll fix you a fancy meal."

She grinned. "Thanks. I'll be dreaming of your fried chicken."

Deuce chuckled. "You take care now." He gave her a final hug and ambled back to stand by Justin. When Justin didn't say anything, Deuce nudged him in the arm.

Justin glanced up at her. "Nice meetin' you, ma'am. I'll keep an eye on Lilly." His gaze darted back to the floor, and his ears turned red.

Mariah smiled. "Thank you. I'm glad to know that."

Deuce nodded at her and then all but shoved Justin back out the door. Fighting a melancholy smile, she jiggled the car keys in her pocket. Her luggage and laptop were already loaded. She'd said her goodbyes to Kelly yesterday and to Hailey before she had left for school earlier.

Now it was time to go home, but she couldn't take the first step toward her car.

Jackson invaded her space, sending her heart into overdrive. He gently rested his chin on her head and sighed. "I wish we'd had more time." His husky voice held a wistful tone.

Mariah closed her eyes. There was nothing she wanted

more than to stay right here and be with Jackson and Hailey for the rest of her life. Even a career as a reporter paled in comparison. She wanted to tell Jackson so badly that she'd given her heart to God, but she knew if she did, he'd ask her to stay. And a man like Jackson deserved someone much better than a person with her history. "I have to go. My deadline is tomorrow."

Jackson took a step back and looked down, his lips pressed into a thin white line. Had something she said hurt him? He seemed upset. After a moment, he sighed again. "I don't suppose it would do any good to ask you not to write your story?"

Mariah gasped. "How could you ask that? You know I have to do my job."

His jaw tightened, and he stared at a window. "We've been through enough here. We don't need the people coming to Angelfire that your story is sure to bring."

"You have no idea what my story says." She lifted up her chin. "I thought you knew me better than to write something that would hurt you."

He shoved his hands in his pockets and turned back, his face cold. "I barely know you at all."

Mariah battled the tears stinging her eyes. The deep ache that settled in her heart sent a shiver through her. Jackson had changed since his fight with Lance. He'd pulled away, and his actions and words were breaking her heart. Just like her father, she couldn't make him love her. "I need to go."

She picked her purse up from the table and hurried to the door, a big part of her wishing she'd never come to Angelfire. Never met Jackson. Because then she wouldn't be missing him already.

Jackson opened his mouth as if he wanted to say something, but Mariah knew if she didn't leave quickly she was going to break down. The pain in his eyes was almost her undoing.

"Mariah, wait—"

"Goodbye, Jackson." She hurried through the mudroom, pushed open the storm door and ran down the porch steps. Inside her car, she twisted on the ignition and threw the transmission into Drive. She carefully avoided Jackson's mangled maple tree and raced the car down the gravel drive with Baron barking his farewell as he ran alongside her. Tears coursed down her cheeks, and she wondered if her heart would ever be free from its pain.

Jackson felt as if someone had impaled him with a sword. Betrayed again. First Misty. Then Lance. And now Mariah. He'd always heard bad things came in threes.

He shoved the storm door open and stepped outside. The dust from Mariah's car was still settling. Wasn't that somehow poetic? He was sure that a long time would pass before the dust from Mariah's visit settled in his heart.

Why did she have to be so stubborn? Was her story— her career—more important to her than him?

Evidently so.

He snorted a cynical laugh.

At least she hadn't left him for another man.

It was better this way. He wasn't marrying material.

A deep loneliness penetrated his being. Jackson sank down on the step, ignoring the cold seeping into his body from the frigid wooden planks. His heart felt as though it would implode. His emotions had been running at full speed, and now a meltdown was coming.

This was all his fault. His marriage to Misty had gone sour before they'd ever reached the end of the first quarter. He never should have allowed his attraction to Mariah to grow. Because now he loved her.

But she'd left him.

Just like Misty.

SEVENTEEN

Mariah closed her Bible and stared out over the railing. She loved having her devotions outside on the apartment's small balcony when the winter temperature was warm enough.

Once again she'd meditated on *Isaiah* 40:31. "But they that wait upon the Lord shall renew their strength; they shall mount up with wings as eagles; they shall run, and not be weary; and they shall walk, and not faint."

She was finding that verse to be true. Each day, the Lord had given her the strength to put one foot in front of the other, even though her heart was still hurting. How could she love a man so much when she'd known him only a short time?

She'd never been one to believe in love at first sight, but her feelings for Jackson came close to that. He was such a good man. She'd met several single men who seemed nice at the church she'd been attending for the past two weeks, but none measured up to Jackson's standard.

She'd thought about calling him and asking if he'd read her article and what he'd thought about it. Had he been pleased with it? At least she'd been in contact with Kelly some, via email. Jackson's sister kept her up-to-date with all that was going on at the ranch. She had also helped her understand some of the more confusing elements of being a new Christian.

She had sworn Kelly to secrecy about her new faith. Kelly had argued with her about wanting to tell Jackson, but Mariah didn't want him to know. He had his life, and she had hers. Her job at the *Observer* was secure for now, and she enjoyed her work.

Still, she wondered why he never called her. Did he think of her as often as she did him? Or had he simply put her out of his mind once he was rid of her, like an annoying fly in the kitchen? Mariah shook her head, frightening a little sparrow that had been twittering on a nearby branch. She had to quit thinking about Jackson. He was a brief, wonderful moment God had blessed her with. A moment that showed her there were good men in this world.

If only somehow things could have worked out for them.

Needing a distraction, she tugged the church bulletin from the pages of her Bible. The Christmas Eve service was tomorrow. This would be Mariah's first Christmas as a Christian. Her heart soared with the newfound love for God.

The God that Jackson had introduced her to.

"Argh! Stop it!" She jumped to her feet so fast her lawn chair buckled and fell back against the sliding glass door with a clatter. "Stop thinking about that man."

She needed something physical to do. A long, hard jog was just the thing.

In a matter of minutes, she'd slipped on her sneakers—the ones that still had a tinge of green horse manure along the edges—pulled her hair back into a ponytail and placed her house key in her pocket. After doing several stretching exercises, she pulled open her front door.

A young John Wayne stood there, complete with cowboy hat and boots. No, not John Wayne. Jackson!

Dark blue eyes framed by long, black lashes stared back at her with a gleaming sparkle. His cowboy hat, pushed back on his forehead, revealed a tan line and his dark hair—longer than it had been when she was at Angelfire—hung across it, just begging her to reach out and straighten it.

His lips tilted in an embarrassed grin, revealing the dimples she loved. "Hi." Jackson leaned against the doorframe, his thumbs stuck in his pants pockets.

"Hi."

His warm gaze traveled over her face, like a man starving for a view of someone he dearly loved. "I've missed you."

All normal lines of communication fled her stunned brain. She opened her mouth but nothing came out. Mariah reached out and poked him in the side.

Jackson squirmed. "Hey, that tickles. What was that for?"

"I…uh…just wanted to make sure you were real. Not just a figment of my imagination."

"So, your imagination has been conjuring up images of me?" His charming smile morphed into a confident smirk. He puffed up his chest.

"What are you doing here?" Mariah's mind had run the gamut of trying to come up with a logical reason for Jackson to be standing on her doorstep. She was batting zero.

"I brought you a Christmas present." He reached around the edge of the door and picked up a decorative bag with thin rope handles on it. A cowboy on horseback rode through a half foot of snow, leading a pack mule carrying a Christmas tree. Crinkled red-and-green tissue paper inside the bag accented the colors of the holly border. A curly ribbon of coordinating colors was tied around one of the handles. This was definitely not a man's handiwork.

"What is it?"

Jackson's grin lit up his whole face. His twinkling eyes matched his blue denim shirt. "Open it and find out."

This was not a good idea. She couldn't shake him from

her mind, and here he was, offering her a present? She remembered their painful parting and took a step back, desperately trying to protect her heart. "I can't accept it, whatever it is."

He shoved the bag toward her. "Just open it. Okay?"

Hopeless to refuse him, she reached out and took the gift, trying hard not to think what touching Jackson's finger had just done to her already addled insides. She swallowed the thick lump in her throat. Having him so near was wonderful torture. "Come in," she said, moving backward until her legs bumped into the couch.

He stepped inside and shut the door. She pulled out the tissue paper and laid it on the arm of the sofa. Inside was something denim-looking. She yanked out the heavy object and gave it a shake. "A jacket?"

If she didn't know better, she'd think Jackson was blushing. Maybe it was just the bad lighting in her entryway.

"I just figured a Texan needed something more Western-looking than the horrible purple thing of yours."

"You don't like my coat?"

He shook his head and grinned. "Too citified for me. So, try it on."

Mariah shook the jacket again until it unfolded, then unsnapped it and slipped her arms inside. "It's perfect! How did you know what size to get?"

"Kelly helped me."

She straightened the front of the fleece-lined jacket, reveling in its instant warmth. "Thanks. I love—" Her hand entered the right pocket and encountered something hard. As she pulled out a small velvet box, her gaze darted to Jackson's.

Could this possibly be what she hoped it was? His dazzling grin sent her hopes soaring as high as an eagle.

"Open it."

With trembling hands, Mariah lifted the black velvet

lid. A beautiful diamond ring glimmered in the light of the sliding glass door. Confusion battled with hope. She looked up at Jackson, hoping for an explanation.

"I read your story in the *Observer*. It was real good." He ducked his head and stared at his boots. "I appreciate your sensitivity in relating what happened with Hailey's kidnapping. And your vagueness about Misty and about where the ranch is located and the fact that you didn't mention its name."

Mariah shrugged, secretly delighted that he was pleased. "Evan was probably upset. My article won't exactly drum up new business."

"He'll get over it."

Jackson's lips tightened into a line and a muscle quivered in his jaw. "I'm sorry for not trusting you. I can make the excuse that I wasn't my normal self with all that had happened, but the truth is, I was afraid."

"Of what—if I can ask?"

He looked in the direction of her balcony, a muscle ticking in his jaw. "I took to heart some of the things Lance said."

She stepped forward, daring to touch his shirt. "No, Jackson. He was a raving madman, and you can't listen to those lies."

He sighed. "I know, but I did at first, and when I came to my senses, I realized I'd just made the biggest mistake of my life when I let you go. My problems with Misty were a result of two immature, selfish people both wanting their own way. It's not that way with us." He cupped her cheek, staring at her with those beautiful eyes. "I may be jumping the gun with the ring, but I felt so certain that you sent me a hidden message when you talked about soaring with the eagles above the storms of life in the article. You've become a Christian."

His gaze, blazing with hope, caught and held hers. Her

heart waltzed with joy. He'd read her article and understood. A smile tugged at her lips that was mirrored by Jackson's.

"Yes. I gave my heart to God."

An expression of pure delight engulfed Jackson's face. "Yeehaw!" He yanked off his hat and threw it in the air. It hit the ceiling and then landed on a blade of the ceiling fan. Jackson grabbed her by the waist and spun her around. It was all she could do to hold on to him and the ring box.

Finally her cowboy gained control of his emotions and set her down. "I'm so happy for you."

"It never would have happened without your example." She stared at the beautiful square diamond encircled with smaller ones. It must have cost a pretty penny. Could she be the wife Jackson needed? She'd grown up with an abusive, alcoholic deadbeat father. She'd never learned how to be a mother or a homemaker. She could only cook things that came from a box. And what about her job? Was she ready to give that up after working so hard to get where she was?

She stared at the worn carpeting and sighed. "Our lives are so different. I—I don't have anything to give you." Glancing up, she begged him with her gaze to understand. "You have everything. A lovely home. A family who adores you. What could I give you that you don't already have?"

"The love and loyalty of a wife fully committed to her husband." His eyes smoldered with longing, and then a cocky smile tilted his lips. "You could also give me a son."

Mariah felt her eyes widen. A son?

A red tinge covered the tips of Jackson's ears. "After we're married, of course."

Wife to Jackson Durant. It was the dream she'd dared not hope could come true. She looked down at the ring in her hand. It was amazing. "I don't know what to say."

"Say you love me. That you'll marry me."

"What about my work?"

"Claremore isn't far away, and there are places online you could write for. If you want to work, I won't hold you back."

She blinked back her tears. Deliriously happy, she couldn't resist the urge to tease him. After all, he had teased her a time or two. She ducked her head in what she hoped was a coy stance and looked up at him through her lashes. "I don't remember you ever asking me to marry you, Jackson Durant."

Something like relief flooded his face right before he chuckled. He tugged on his pant leg and bent down on one knee. "I love you more than I can find the words to express it. Will you marry me, Mariah? Be my wife and the mother of our children?"

Mariah bit her lip, not believing this was really happening. Her tears blurred Jackson's handsome, hopeful face.

"Well?" he said.

"Of course I'll marry you. Yes! Yes! I'll marry you."

Jackson bolted to his feet and took her in his arms. "Oh, darlin', I've missed you so much. I thought I'd died when you left. Probably would have if not for the Lord—that and the fact I had Hailey to care for. Did you know I loved you back then?"

Mariah shrugged. "You said so in Lance's barn, but I thought maybe it was just because emotions were running so high then. I didn't want to believe it might be true. I felt sure I had nothing to offer you."

He pushed her back and looked her in the eye. "Don't ever say that again. I'd have never made it through Hailey's kidnapping without you by my side. Your steady, silent support kept me going. You and God. We made a great trio."

Tears coursed down Mariah's cheeks. Never in her life had she been so happy. Jackson leaned down, and his lips captured hers in a long, lingering kiss. She soared above the clouds, flying high with the eagles.

God had given Mariah her ultimate dream—the only man she'd ever loved. The only man she'd ever cried over.

But even more, God had come into her life. And now He was giving her a place to call home. A daughter to mother. And a cowboy to love.

Her life was complete.

EPILOGUE

"No. Absolutely not! There's no way I'm letting you buy that purple coat for Hailey." Jackson shoved his hands to his hips.

Mariah almost laughed at the adamant expression on her husband's face. "But, honey, you know how much she loved my old lavender jacket." She blinked her eyes, hoping her look portrayed innocence.

"Puh-lease?" Hailey leaned against his side, holding her laced fingers against her chin.

He crossed his arms over the solid chest that Mariah loved to lean against. "No."

"Aw, come on, Dad," Hailey chimed in, holding up a tinier version of the coat. "We could even get a matching one for Hannah."

At hearing her name, Hannah squealed from her stroller and kicked her feet.

"I'm not having this conversation." Jackson turned away and marched across the aisle to the hardware section.

Hailey's laughter joined Mariah's.

After she and Jackson had been married several months, she'd walked outside one day wearing her lavender jacket. He'd scowled and stormed toward her, stripped the coat off

her back and threw it in the bonfire, where he was burning
leaves. "Cowgirls don't wear purple coats," he'd mumbled.

Mariah had been stunned at his odd behavior. She still
remembered standing there with her mouth hanging open.
His action was so out of character for her sweet, gentle husband. After her initial shock had worn off, she had grabbed
her stomach and laughed until tears ran down her cheeks.

Looking chagrined, Jackson had walked toward her, head
hanging. "I guess I kind of overreacted. Sorry." He pulled
off his hat and smacked it against his leg. "It's just that I
hate that jacket. It's so—so citified. Makes you look like
a greenhorn."

That memory was one of Mariah's favorites.

Now she fluffed Hannah's dark hair, so much like her
father's, and watched as ten-year-old Hailey walked toward
a group of her friends. Hannah whined for her daddy and
tried to climb out of her stroller. Mariah held her bulging
belly and bent down, ready to pick up her daughter.

"I'll get her." Jackson jogged back across the aisle. "You
know the doctor told you not to lift Hannah until after Buck
is born."

"I am not naming my son Buck." She glared, daring him
to argue with her. This wasn't the first time they'd had this
playful conversation.

"Buck. Elmer. Billy Bob. Whatever." Jackson's teasing
grin still sent butterflies dancing in her stomach. "Just so
long as he's healthy, it doesn't matter."

"Jackson Jr."

"We'll see," he said, but his proud grin said otherwise.
"You 'bout ready to go eat? I'm dying for one of Marvin's
big, thick steaks."

She nodded, her mouth already salivating for a juicy rib
eye. With Hannah in one arm, Jackson wrapped his other
arm around her shoulders, and she leaned against him.

Would she always be this happy?

Probably not, but walking with God was like flying with the eagles. The storms of life would continue to pummel her, but with God's help, she would rise above the tumultuous times and sail high on eagles' wings.

* * * * *

Dear Reader,

Writing a contemporary suspense was a big one-eighty from the historical novels I normally pen. I thoroughly enjoyed raining havoc on Jackson and Mariah and throwing a country guy and city gal together and watching what happened. I've always loved stories about strong but hurting heroes, and Jackson's story was begging to be told.

Mariah endured a difficult childhood that altered her opinion of men and God. Through Jackson's wonderful example of a man strong in faith and a father who dearly loves his child, she sees that there are good men in this world, and she learns how to fly above the storms of life.

None of us venture through life unscathed, but I hope *Rancher Under Fire* helped you to see how you can face the storms of life head-on and soar above them with God's help. I hope you enjoyed *Rancher Under Fire* and will check out my other books. I love hearing from readers, so if you wish to send me a note, you can contact me via my website, www.vickiemcdonough.com.

God's blessings on your life,
Vickie McDonough

Questions for Discussion

1. Jackson had lived life in the fast lane, enjoying all that comes with being a popular pro quarterback. When he moved to the ranch, his life totally changed. What type of difficulties do you think he encountered? Have you faced hardships when making a big change in your life?

2. Mariah was desperate to get her story. As she got to know Jackson, she began to waver in her determination. Have you ever had to make a difficult choice that could drastically affect someone else? How did you handle that decision?

3. Lance was Jackson's best friend. Do you think Jackson was naive to not realize Lance was the source of his problems? Were there signs of Lance's behavior that he should have picked up on but didn't because of their friendship?

4. Mariah was determined to get her story, but the one she ended up writing wasn't what she'd first planned. What changed her mind?

5. Jackson had a loving, close-knit family but Mariah didn't. How did the differences affect them? How did it shape their character?

6. Toward the end of the story, Mariah decides she wants a faith in God like Jackson has. What things held her back from making that choice sooner?

7. How did Jackson's example of a godly man move Mariah forward in wanting a relationship with God?

8. Discuss what keeps you from trusting God or believing in His goodness.

9. When Hailey was missing, Jackson never stopped believing God would keep her safe and return her to him. What does it take to have such a strong faith in God during tragic times?

10. Jackson used eagles and their abilities to help Mariah understand about God and how he protects us. Talk about a time when God protected you.

11. Mariah felt like a fish out of water at Angelfire Ranch, but she kept learning new things and adapting. Was there a time you felt the same? How did you handle the situation?

12. What do you think about how Jackson talked about his faith? Did he come on too strong?

13. When the barn caught fire, Mariah's first thought was to get Hailey out. How do you react when an emergency hits? Do you jump into action or cower in the corner?

14. Did you suspect Lance was the person causing Jackson's problems? If not, whom did you suspect and why? If so, what made you suspect he was the culprit?

15. Jackson told Mariah that with God's help, we can soar

above the storms like an eagle. Has there been a troubling time in your life when you were able to soar above the difficulties?

COMING NEXT MONTH FROM
Love Inspired® Suspense

Available October 7, 2014

THE LAWMAN RETURNS
Wrangler's Corner • by Lynette Eason

When his brother is murdered, deputy Clay Starke is determined to find the killer. Could beautiful social worker Sabrina Mayfield hold the missing clue?

DOWN TO THE WIRE
SWAT: Top Cops • by Laura Scott

Someone has planted a bomb under schoolteacher Tess Collins's desk and only explosives expert Declan Shaw can save her. Together they must figure out how she became the obsession of a madman before she becomes the next victim.

HOLIDAY DEFENDERS
by Debby Giusti, Susan Sleeman and Jodie Bailey

When danger strikes at Christmastime, these military heroes are ready to give their all for their country—and for the women they love.

COVERT CHRISTMAS
Echo Mountain • by Hope White

Search and Rescue K-9 dog handler Breanna McBride witnesses Scott Becket getting shot and comes to his aid. Realizing he has amnesia, Breanna and Scott try and retrace his steps to remember his past, but soon discover some things are better left forgotten....

TUNDRA THREAT • by Sarah Varland
When McKenna Clark stumbles across a double homicide in the Alaskan tundra, the wildlife trooper knows she's in over her head. But that doesn't mean she'll let former crush Will Harrison help with the investigation—until they find that *she's* become the attacker's new target.

KEEPING WATCH • by Jane M. Choate
Someone is stalking Danielle Barclay, and her bodyguard, former Delta Force soldier Jake Rabb, will stop at nothing to keep her safe. Even if it means putting his own life in danger.

LISCNM0914

REQUEST YOUR FREE BOOKS!

2 FREE RIVETING INSPIRATIONAL NOVELS
PLUS 2 FREE MYSTERY GIFTS

Love Inspired®
SUSPENSE

YES! Please send me 2 FREE Love Inspired® Suspense novels and my 2 FREE mystery gifts (gifts are worth about $10). After receiving them, if I don't wish to receive any more books, I can return the shipping statement marked "cancel." If I don't cancel, I will receive 4 brand-new novels every month and be billed just $4.74 per book in the U.S. or $5.24 per book in Canada. That's a savings of at least 21% off the cover price. It's quite a bargain! Shipping and handling is just 50¢ per book in the U.S. and 75¢ per book in Canada.* I understand that accepting the 2 free books and gifts places me under no obligation to buy anything. I can always return a shipment and cancel at any time. Even if I never buy another book, the two free books and gifts are mine to keep forever.

123/323 IDN F5AC

Name _____ (PLEASE PRINT) _____

Address _____ Apt. # _____

City _____ State/Prov. _____ Zip/Postal Code _____

Signature (if under 18, a parent or guardian must sign)

Mail to the Harlequin® Reader Service:
IN U.S.A.: P.O. Box 1867, Buffalo, NY 14240-1867
IN CANADA: P.O. Box 609, Fort Erie, Ontario L2A 5X3

**Are you a current subscriber to Love Inspired Suspense books
and want to receive the larger-print edition?
Call 1-800-873-8635 or visit www.ReaderService.com.**

* Terms and prices subject to change without notice. Prices do not include applicable taxes. Sales tax applicable in N.Y. Canadian residents will be charged applicable taxes. Offer not valid in Quebec. This offer is limited to one order per household. Not valid for current subscribers to Love Inspired Suspense books. All orders subject to credit approval. Credit or debit balances in a customer's account(s) may be offset by any other outstanding balance owed by or to the customer. Please allow 4 to 6 weeks for delivery. Offer available while quantities last.

Your Privacy—The Harlequin® Reader Service is committed to protecting your privacy. Our Privacy Policy is available online at www.ReaderService.com or upon request from the Harlequin Reader Service.
We make a portion of our mailing list available to reputable third parties that offer products we believe may interest you. If you prefer that we not exchange your name with third parties, or if you wish to clarify or modify your communication preferences, please visit us at www.ReaderService.com/consumerchoice or write to us at Harlequin Reader Service Preference Service, P.O. Box 9062, Buffalo, NY 14269. Include your complete name and address.

LIS13R

Love Inspired
SUSPENSE
RIVETING INSPIRATIONAL ROMANCE

AROUND-THE-CLOCK PROTECTOR

Despite the threats against her life, Danielle Barclay thinks having a bodyguard is unnecessary. Or at least that's what she tells herself before meeting Jake Rabb. A former Delta Force solider, Jake is used to rope-lining from helicopters into enemy territory–not following around a senator's daughter. The lovely deputy district attorney is as strong-willed as she is brave, especially when the escalating danger assures Jake that her stalker means business. As the attacks become personal, Danielle finally puts her trust–and her feelings–on the line with her defender. But how will Jake protect her if the stalker is closer than they think?

KEEPING WATCH
by
JANE M. CHOATE

**Available October 2014 wherever
Love Inspired books and ebooks are sold.**

LIS44629